PLAYING WITH FIRE

"Jessica, you've been out with Bruce all this time?"

"Oh, yes," Jessica said ecstatically. "And it was wonderful!"

"I was afraid of that."

"Afraid? I can handle myself just fine. Why can't you get it into your thick skull that Bruce likes me!"

"It takes more than a few kisses to prove that," Elizabeth declared to her sister.

"Look, if there's something specific you have to tell me about him, go ahead."

"He's arrogant and self-centered. He'll hurt you."

Jessica snorted. "Just what I thought. You don't have any real reasons—just your own opinions. Sorry, Liz, but you're going to have to do better than that." She stormed out of the room.

Elizabeth stood alone in front of the dresser, her eyes brimming with tears. She was sure that Bruce Patman was just playing another game with her unsuspecting sister. And she was almost as sure it was a game Jessica couldn't win.

SWEET VALLEY HIGH

PLAYING WITH FIRE

Written by
Kate William

Created by
FRANCINE PASCAL

BANTAM BOOKS
TORONTO · NEW YORK · LONDON · SYDNEY · AUCKLAND

RL 6, IL age 12 and up

PLAYING WITH FIRE

A Bantam Book / December 1983

2nd printing	... February 1984	5th printing	.... January 1985
3rd printing	...... May 1984	6th printing	.... June 1985
4th printing	... September 1984	7th printing	... September 1985
	8th printing	...... March 1986	

Sweet Valley High is a trademark of Francine Pascal

Conceived by Francine Pascal

Produced by Cloverdale Press, Inc.

Cover art by James Mathewuse

ISBN 0-553-25034-5

Published simultaneously in the United States and Canada

Bantam Books are published by Bantam Books, Inc. Its trademark,
consisting of the words "Bantam Books" and the portrayal of a rooster,
is Registered in U.S. Patent and Trademark Office and in other
countries. Marca Registrada. Bantam Books, Inc., 666 Fifth Avenue,
New York, New York 10103.

PLAYING WITH FIRE

One

"Well, if it isn't her royal highness herself." Todd Wilkins gently nudged Elizabeth Wakefield's shoulder and pointed toward the entrance to the school gymnasium.

Elizabeth peered into the crowd that had already assembled for the Sweet Valley High dance contest. She sighed with relief when she spotted the person Todd was talking about—her twin sister, Jessica. With the contest only minutes away, Elizabeth had begun to worry about Jessica, even though it wasn't the first time her twin had shown up late to an important event. Casting a concerned look back in her boyfriend's direction, Elizabeth murmured, "I wonder where Jessica was all this time."

"Really, Liz." Todd shook his head in mock

1

exasperation. "You know Jessica always waits until everyone's gathered to make her grand entrance."

"You're exaggerating, Todd," Elizabeth replied defensively, although silently she admitted there was some truth to Todd's words. Jessica had always said that a party never really started until she got there, and this occasion appeared to be the perfect time to prove her point. Already a small crowd had begun to form around the popular blonde. "Anyway, so what if Jess likes to shine in the spotlight?" Elizabeth added. "She *was* elected fall queen, you know, and royalty's entitled to certain privileges. Besides, she's not hurting anyone, is she?"

"No—except maybe the king," Todd noted pointedly.

About six paces behind Jessica stood Winston Egbert, Sweet Valley High's fall king and Jessica's date for the evening. Elizabeth would have liked to say something to explain away her sister's lack of concern for Winston, but she held her tongue, refusing to get into yet another fight over Jessica. Her twin was the only sore spot in Elizabeth's relationship with Todd. He still hadn't forgiven Jessica for the time she'd made him think Elizabeth wasn't interested in him, and Elizabeth saw no point in making the situation worse.

Besides, Elizabeth was well aware just how *un*thrilled Jessica was at having to spend the evening with Winston, for Elizabeth had spent the

2

better part of her afternoon listening to her sister moan and groan about it. According to school tradition, the fall queen was supposed to accompany the king to certain school-sponsored activities during the semester. There was no way Jessica could get out of it, short of giving up her crown—and all the glory that went with it. It wasn't that she didn't like Winston, she'd carefully explained to her twin sister. Who at Sweet Valley didn't? He was always smiling, always joking—something of a class clown—yet in his own way one of the more interesting boys in school. It was who he *wasn't* that bothered Jessica. He wasn't Bruce Patman, the boy she longed to be with, the boy she'd hoped to snag when she'd schemed to be elected queen. The fact that Bruce still eluded her was a constant source of torment to Jessica. She always got what she wanted, and she hadn't yet met a boy who could resist her for very long. She desperately hoped Bruce wasn't turning out to be the exception.

Jessica was getting impatient. She'd been secretly in love with Bruce for years. He was good-looking and charming—and his family was one of the most prominent and richest in Sweet Valley, which made him even more attractive to her. But Jessica's frustration had begun to mount almost immediately as she'd watched him go after nearly every girl on the A list at school.

Every girl, it seemed, but her.

Jessica was already chatting with Cara Walker and a few of her other Pi Beta Alpha sorority sisters by the time Winston reached her side. There was a look of admiration on his face.

Dressed in a bright blue, skin-hugging mini-dress and matching tights, Jessica was an eye-catching sight. The outfit accented her long, shapely legs and brought out the blue in her sparkling aquamarine eyes. Across the room, Elizabeth, in her stylish but more casual wheat-colored pants and tan, striped shirt, also eyed her twin with admiration. Blessed with the same all-American blond good looks, the sisters appeared as alike as identical twins possibly could, but Elizabeth some-times envied what she felt was her sister's more dramatic flair.

The floor of the gym was dotted with couples keeping pace with the rhythmic beat of The Droids, whose frenetic tempo and catchy original tunes made them Sweet Valley High's most popular band. Dana Larson, the group's lead singer, was in the middle of their latest song, "I've Found Paradise." The lyrics told how her Eden would be complete only when she found the right boy to share it with. Elizabeth mused that with as many guys as there were hooked on Dana's miniskirted figure, exotically styled short blond hair, and tantalizing voice, the singer would have no trouble making that wish come true.

"Hey, Todd, do you know who that guy is?"

Elizabeth asked. She pointed to a tall, lanky man in his early twenties standing at the back of the gym near the bleachers. He was dressed in red leather pants, with a matching skinny tie knotted loosely over his white shirt. He was staring intently at the stage and seemed absorbed in the music.

"Nah, never saw him before," Todd answered. "Maybe he's Ms. Dalton's new boyfriend."

"I doubt it. Since we've been here, he hasn't been near her. He's handsome enough for her, though."

Todd grinned. "I'm sure your reporter's instincts will sniff out the truth by the end of the evening. C'mon, let's wish Jess good luck on the contest. She's going to need it 'cause she's in for some tough competition."

"Oh, really? From whom?" Elizabeth asked.

Todd pointed to the ground. "These feet were born to dance. And my partner's not exactly clumsy, either. I heard somewhere that identical twins have identical talents."

"Jessica and I aren't identical in every way—as *you* should certainly know," Elizabeth said airily, shrugging off Todd's challenge. "Look, if we're going to see Jess, we'd better hurry. The contest will be starting anytime now."

Jessica lit up in a wide smile at the sight of her sister. "Hi, Liz," she said, beaming. "Having a good time?"

5

"Don't I always?" Elizabeth answered brightly. Then she turned to her sister's date. "You ready for the contest, Win?"

"Are you kidding?" He did a quick shuffle, nearly tripping over his gangly legs. "After tonight we go on to *Dance Fever*. Right, Jessica?"

Jessica, who had been scanning the room snapped back into the conversation at the sound of her name. "Oh, sure—whatever you say, Win." Turning to Elizabeth and Todd, she added, "By the way, you haven't seen Bruce Patman around, have you?"

"As a matter of fact, yes," Todd replied. "Over by the bleachers, surrounded by the usual horde of girls dying to get near him. Why do you ask?"

"Oh, nothing important." Jessica tossed her head as if to dismiss the subject, but her tone was a little too light to be totally believable. "I just wanted to wish him good luck tonight."

Elizabeth shot her sister a warning look. *How can she talk about Bruce with Win standing right next to her?* she thought angrily. "I hope he doesn't upstage you, little sister," Elizabeth said, using the affectionate nickname she had long ago given Jessica because she was four minutes younger than Elizabeth was. "I know how much winning this contest means to you."

"Oh, I'm not worried about that, big sister," Jessica declared. "Just remember what we talked about this afternoon—and don't blow it, OK, Lizzie?''

Elizabeth was saddened by the urgency she heard in Jessica's voice. Earlier in the day Jessica had practically begged her not to try to win the contest, but Elizabeth hadn't taken her seriously. Jessica simply never begged for anything. But now she could see that her sister meant every word. *She'll really do anything to attract Bruce's attention*, Elizabeth suddenly realized. Glancing at Todd for a moment, she avoided Jessica's stare, then replied noncommittally, "I'll remember, and I'll see."

The high-pitched voice of Robin Wilson cut abruptly into their conversation. "Jessica! What an incredible dress! I love it! Where did you get it? I've got to get one just like it!" A recent arrival to Sweet Valley, Robin had quickly attached herself to Jessica. Robin had the unfortunate tendency to show up at the most inopportune times. Such as that moment.

"Cool it, Robin. I get your point," Jessica said, giving the overweight girl one of her fake, bright smiles, while thinking the last thing in the world she'd want was to be seen in the same outfit as Miss Tubby. "Oops, there's Lila. I've got to talk to her." Jessica quickly excused herself. Turning to Elizabeth, she added, "I'll catch up with you later. You're going up to Ken's, aren't you?"

"Wouldn't miss it for anything. Ken always throws the greatest parties."

7

"Ta-ta, then." And with that she ran off.

"Party? What party?" Robin asked, running after Jessica as fast as her plump legs would carry her.

But Jessica was off like a frenetic butterfly to huddle with her friend Lila Fowler. *She's probably getting tips on how to snare Bruce Patman*, Elizabeth thought worriedly, fearing that her sister's apparent single-mindedness might force her to do anything to get him. Lila had had a brief fling with the handsome, dark-haired senior some months earlier and considered herself an expert on him.

The dance contest was about to begin. The Droids had finished up their set, and as the lights dimmed, Roger Collins bounded onto the stage. Looking as handsome as a rock star, but dressed conservatively in comfortable, well-worn cords and a sweater, the popular, good-looking teacher positioned his lean frame behind the microphone. He clearly enjoyed his role as chaperon for the dance. "Good evening, ladies and gentlemen," he began grandly.

"Good evening, Mr. Collins," they all singsonged back at him in unison, affectionately mocking his master-of-ceremonies act.

Smiling broadly, Mr. Collins continued. "Welcome to Sweet Valley's Fifth Annual Rockin' Dance Party Contest. You all having a good time tonight?"

The crowd answered with a roar.

"Great!" he cried. "You know the rules. The

band will play three songs. While our contestants dance, the judges will circulate around the floor, and after a short break the winners will be announced." Pausing a moment for effect, Mr. Collins smiled at his audience, which was practically squirming with anticipation. "OK, then! Let's get started! Per Sweet Valley tradition, we'll lead off the contest with our king and queen. So without further ado, I present to you King Winston Egbert and Queen Jessica Wakefield."

A lone spotlight focused on the couple as The Droids let loose with a fast, wall-shaking number. Jessica was clearly in her element, moving with the music naturally and without effort. Even her lustrous golden hair swayed to the beat, completing the perfect picture of a dancer caught up in ecstasy.

Unfortunately for Jessica and her dreams of placing first, she had to share the spotlight with Winston. That's where the perfect picture ended. He was a very clumsy dancer, trying to hide his ineptness by acting like a clown.

As they danced, Jessica's expression went from happiness to pure, helpless fury as she watched Winston run in circles around her, comically kicking his feet and clapping his hands. With the way Winston was carrying on, she realized, there was no way she'd ever win the contest, even if Elizabeth—who *was* as good a dancer as her twin—held back a little.

Halfway through the first dance, in an act of quiet desperation, Jessica made heavy eye contact with a strikingly handsome boy. To her surprise and enormous delight, he caught her mental SOS and began to walk in her direction.

Jessica's pulse quickened. *He's coming*, she thought excitedly, not quite believing her eyes. *Bruce Patman is coming to dance with me!* She was so overcome by the very thought that she stopped moving—and Winston immediately stepped on her foot.

"I'm so sorry, Jessica," he apologized.

Jessica snapped back to attention. "It's OK. I'm used to it," she grumbled. "But what are you trying to do, put me in the hospital?"

Before Winston could reply, Bruce tapped his shoulder. "I've been watching your moves, Egbert, and I think you could use a little help. Watch how I do it." In one smooth move Bruce pulled Jessica from the startled Winston and took her in his arms.

Bruce got no argument from Winston. He knew when he was upstaged. Accepting the inevitable, he quietly slunk to the refreshment table at the side of the gym.

With conflicting emotions, Elizabeth had watched the scene unfold. Her sister did deserve to win, but it hardly seemed worth hurting Winston to get the prize. Especially if, as Elizabeth suspected, the prize was Bruce. "Well, would you look at that!" she said to Todd, nodding toward Jessica's new partner.

"I'm not surprised. Jessica always gets what she wants."

"Bruce Patman." Elizabeth mouthed the name of the one boy she'd hoped Jessica would never catch. "I wonder what brought this on?" she said aloud. "What does that egomaniac want with Jessica?"

"Looks simple enough to me," Todd remarked. "The guy wants to win the contest—and Jessica's his best hope. I'm sure that's all it is."

Elizabeth hoped that Todd was right, and she had to admit that Bruce was as good a dancer as Jessica. Together they moved across the floor as if they'd always been partners.

When the first dance ended, they were clearly unwilling to separate; and during the second and third songs Bruce and Jessica shifted into more complex moves. With the strength of his well-muscled body, Bruce lifted Jessica high in the air and spun her around his broad shoulders and across his body. They were pure grace, electricity in motion, and as more and more couples grew aware of what they were up against, they dropped out of the contest to stand aside and admire this masterful performance. By the time the third song ended, only a handful of couples remained—and the outcome of the contest was certain.

Even Mr. Collins didn't try to prolong the suspense when he stepped back on stage to announce the winners. "Jessica Wakefield and Bruce Patman, come on up here and get your award." To a smattering of applause the handsome couple accepted the trophy from Mr. Collins. "Now you can lead everyone in the next dance."

Elizabeth was sure that the smile on Jessica's face had little to do with winning the contest. It appeared she'd won what she considered a more valuable prize—Bruce Patman. But Elizabeth couldn't force herself to share her sister's happiness. She knew the real Bruce better than Jessica did. Back on the dance floor, Bruce had wrapped Jessica tightly in his arms as they moved in time to a slow ballad. She held on to him as if she were living a dream she was afraid would end at any moment.

"You're some dancer, Bruce," she whispered breathlessly. "A big improvement over Win—especially on these slow numbers."

"Glad you noticed, baby," he murmured sweetly. "Anyway, slow dancing isn't really dancing."

"What do you mean, Bruce?"

"It's just the easiest way for a guy to get his arms around a girl."

"Oh? Is that the only reason you picked me for a partner tonight?" Jessica pretended to pout.

"It's a good reason—and I do have my arms around you."

"And I have mine around you. I'd say it works

for both sexes," she retorted, pulling her body closer to his in typical Jessica Wakefield fashion.

But Bruce pushed her back ever so slightly. "In dancing, at least, the guy still takes the lead."

His meaning wasn't lost on Jessica. She'd have to be less aggressive if she wanted to keep him interested. "Then I'll follow wherever you lead," she said with uncharacteristic submissiveness. Bruce nudged closer and rubbed his hand approvingly over the nape of her neck.

Over at the refreshment table Winston downed his fifth cola as he stared disconsolately at the dance floor. Elizabeth, hoping to cheer him up, poured herself a root beer and sauntered over to him. "For a guy who's usually in the middle of everything, you're pretty quiet tonight," she remarked.

Winston pasted a broad smile on his face. "Just taking a time out. We kings have a heavy schedule."

Elizabeth wasn't fooled by his false show of bravado. "Don't let Jessica get you down, Win. She's always doing things first and thinking about them later."

"You talking about her and Patman? No big deal," he said lightly. "Why shouldn't she want to dance with someone who doesn't step all over her toes?"

"Come on, Win. I saw you! You could be good if you tried."

Smiling appreciatively at Elizabeth, he put down

his drink. "Look, the dance is almost over. Once it is, she'll dump Bruce and come back to me. We're still going to Ken's party together."

"I see," she said, with a look that expressed her doubts.

"Hey, don't worry about me," Winston added. "I can handle your sister just fine."

"I sure hope so, Win," Elizabeth said, trying to sound supportive. In her sixteen years she'd yet to come across a boy who could truly control her tempestuous twin.

After The Droids finished their last set, Elizabeth noticed that the mysterious man in the red leather pants was talking animatedly with them. Jessica and Bruce were still in the middle of the dance floor, moving to music only they could hear. In an effort to divert Winston's attention from this scene, Elizabeth steered him into a discussion about whether the Sweet Valley Gladiators had a chance at the state football championship this year. At first Winston talked freely, but when he realized what Elizabeth was doing, he stood up straight and announced, "Excuse me, Liz, but I've got something important to do."

"Win, wait!" Elizabeth called. But Winston wasn't listening.

Elizabeth was about to go after him when she felt a tap on her shoulder. "Got a second?"

She turned to face Emily Mayer, The Droids' drummer. "I may have a scoop for your column,"

14

Emily said, casually running a hand through her dark brown, wavy hair. She was referring to the "Eyes and Ears" column Elizabeth wrote for the school paper. "It's not official yet, but it looks like you've just seen our last high school concert."

Elizabeth couldn't hide her shock. "You mean you guys are splitting up?"

"Oh, no! What I mean is—The Droids are going big time!"

"What are you talking about?"

"This guy came up to us after we finished our set." Emily was racing now, trying to get the words out as fast as she could. "He wants to manage us. He says he could make us stars!"

"The guy in the red pants?"

Emily nodded.

"Are you sure he's for real?" Elizabeth asked skeptically.

"I know it sounds crazy, but he's legit, Liz. His name is Tony Conover, and he's a representative of T.G. Goode and Associates. That may not mean anything to you, but they're the agency that books all the major clubs in L.A. Tony said he's the one who discovered August Moon and the Savage Six, and look where they are now. He's been scouting around the entire state looking at bands just like ours, and he says we've got what it takes."

"It sounds impressive," Elizabeth agreed. "But don't rush into anything too quickly. I mean, isn't it all kind of sudden?"

"Look," Emily said with a trace of annoyance, "we're not going to do anything without giving it careful thought. But just think, Liz, soon we could be playing L.A.!"

Elizabeth grinned. "I'll be there when you do!"

Moments later Elizabeth caught up with Todd, and together they rushed to the edge of the bleachers, where Jessica and Winston were in a heated discussion.

"Look, Win, all I'm saying is that I just can't spend the rest of the evening with you!" Jessica shouted.

"But, Jess, we had a date for tonight."

"Just because we came here together doesn't mean we have to leave together. Where's your sense of adventure, Win? C'mon, loosen up. *You're* free to do whatever *you* want."

"I want to be with you."

"Well, *almost* anything you want." Jessica's eyes lit up in inspiration. "I've got it! Why don't you take Robin Wilson to Ken's place? She'd love it. Oh, the two of you would be just perfect." Then, as if everything were now happily resolved, Jessica patted Winston on the shoulder. "See you, Win. And thanks for being such a good sport."

"Sure—anytime," he mumbled to her retreating back.

Elizabeth had heard enough. Leaving Todd to

16

cheer up the defeated Winston, she raced to her sister's side before Jessica had a chance to find Bruce.

"Hold it, Jessica."

Elizabeth didn't use such a commanding tone very often, and Jessica always knew when her sister spoke that way it had to be something serious. She stopped and turned. "What is it, Liz?"

"How could you do that to Win? You've humiliated him."

"Oh, that. He'll get over it," she answered breezily. "It's not like we're a couple or anything."

"No, but you had a date with him tonight."

"So what? Where does it say I have to chain myself to Koko the Clown all night? I've been waiting for Bruce since—since birth, for heaven's sake! If you think I'm going to let him go now, you're wrong!"

"But do you really think he's for you?" Elizabeth persisted.

"Actually, yes. I think he's perfect."

"I'm telling you, Jess—"

"Lizzie, that's enough," Jessica hissed. "You've done your big-sister number. Now it's time to leave me alone."

"But, Jess—"

"I said forget it, Liz. It's none of your business. I've got to find Bruce." She peered into the group of kids milling around the outside door to the

17

gym. Seeing him, her heart melted, and her voice grew noticeably softer. "There he is now. Hey, Bruce, wait for me," she called into the crowd.

With that, Jessica floated into the waiting arms of the most desirable boy at Sweet Valley High.

And all Elizabeth could do was shake her head and hope she was wrong about Bruce. For her sister's sake.

Two

Elizabeth couldn't keep from biting her nails on the way to Ken's party. She wanted to keep an eye on Jessica just in case her sister got too carried away. Turning to Todd, she snapped impatiently, "Can't you make this car go faster?"

"Hey, what's with you? The party's just getting started." He turned to her and frowned when he noticed the worried expression on her face. "Oh, I get it. It's Jessica, isn't it?"

"Yes, it's Jessica," Elizabeth admitted. "I don't think she knows what she's getting herself into."

Todd shook his head. "Seems to me she's going to do what she wants anyway, Liz. You can't be her mother."

"I know, but if she'd only listen to me, maybe I could keep her from getting hurt."

19

"By Bruce?" Todd snickered. "Jessica's a big girl. She can handle herself just fine without your help. Besides, I'd say Bruce is the one who should be careful. Not that I think it's necessary. They seem perfect for each other."

"Jessica's feelings are sincere. I wish I could say as much about Bruce's."

"Since when have you become an expert on the inner workings of Bruce Patman? Isn't it possible he could like your sister?"

"Anything's possible," she conceded.

"So what's the problem?"

"The problem is that Jess has had a secret crush on Bruce for practically forever. And she wasn't acting like herself at all tonight. It was weird. When she just heard Bruce's name, she looked as if she were ready to fall at his feet. I'm afraid of what might happen. I don't think he's good for her. He's not a nice guy, and I don't want to see her get hurt. I can tell she thinks he's a dream come true, and it scares me."

Todd turned into the long, winding dirt road to Ken's lakeside house, then parked beside a number of other cars that had transformed the Matthewses' neat grounds into a miniature parking lot. "How are you going to stop her?"

"I don't know for sure," she said dejectedly as she got out of the car. Then she smiled. "But I certainly don't want to ruin your evening, Todd, figuring it out." Arm in arm they approached the crowd gathering behind the stately stone-faced house.

It didn't take her long to spot Jessica, who, to Elizabeth's dismay, had her arm locked securely around Bruce's waist. The new couple was standing on the patio talking to Ken and his date, Lila Fowler, and Paul Sherwood and a few of Bruce's other friends from the tennis team—a group Elizabeth thought were cliquey snobs. Jessica was staring adoringly into Bruce's deep blue eyes. Elizabeth knew that her twin, who was usually in total control of herself, would die if she could see how she was behaving now, but she also realized that this was not the time to confront Jessica. A big scene in front of this crowd could be a disaster.

Sighing, she allowed Todd to steer her toward another group gathered near the lake.

Jessica, meanwhile, had to keep pinching herself to believe she was really there with Bruce. Totally oblivious to the conversation taking place, her mind kept repeating the words he'd whispered while they'd been dancing. *"I've had my eyes on you for a long time, Jess. We could have a real good time together."*

As always, Bruce was enjoying being the center of attention and enthusiastically reenacted an incident that had occurred the night before. ". . . So I looked behind me, and there's the big red light of a cop car gaining on me. I could have put my black beauty into fifth and really let her rip, but I was in a generous mood, so I pulled off to the side of the road. 'What's the matter, officer?' I asked. I was really polite, trying to get on his good side. But he wasn't buying. 'Gimme your license and registration'—he was really barking at me, you know? The guy was mean, the type who'd put you in a choke hold without blinking an eye. So I gave him the stuff, and he says, 'Hmm, Patman, eh?' He's no fool, he knows the name, so I say, 'Yeah, Patman. One of the Sweet Valley Patmans. What of it?' 'Uh, Mr. Patman'—he called me *mister*, can you believe it?—'you were going eighty-two in a thirty-five zone.' So I say, 'That's too bad. I'll try not to do that anymore.' Then I flashed a twenty under his nose. 'What do you say we just pretend this never happened?' And you know, he took it! You ought to try that the next time *you* get caught, Kenny boy.''

"Maybe I would if my name were Patman," he answered. "You sure you didn't threaten to sic your dad on this guy?"

"Now, would I do a thing like that?" Bruce asked with mock indignation. "I'm too nice a guy to stoop to that, wouldn't you say, Jessica?" He squeezed her around the waist.

A long silence followed as everyone in the group waited for Jessica's reply. Finally, realizing all eyes were upon her, she snapped out of her daydream. "Oh, am I supposed to say something?" she asked.

22

For the first time in her life, she was caught completely off guard.

Lila looked at her with undisguised amusement. Well aware of Jessica's crush on Bruce, she could see that her friend was already off the deep end. *Good luck, Jess*, she thought. *You're going to need it.*

Ken, feeling embarrassed for Jessica, stepped in to rescue her. "I think it's time we all cooled off. What do you say we get our suits and hop in the lake?"

After changing into a bright red bikini that accented every curve of her trim body, Jessica joined Bruce at the lake's edge. Though the night was warm, she shivered. Was it the temperature—or the sight of Bruce's own lean, firm frame? She wasn't certain. The sensation was thrilling, nevertheless, and it was heightened when she watched Bruce dive gracefully into the water. *He's beautiful*, she thought, aware of a tense stirring inside her. The first feelings of love, she was sure of it. Confidently she positioned herself on the diving platform and did a perfect backflip into the deep, cool water.

When she surfaced, Bruce was by her side. "Pretty fancy move there, babe," he remarked, impressed.

"I was on the girls' swim team in junior high,"

she reminded him proudly as they swam to a point where the water was no longer over their heads. They both stood, a bit apart from each other. The shock of the cool water had done little to ease the tension within Jessica. Only the touch of Bruce's arms, she realized, could soothe her now. She swam a few strokes and stopped very close to him.

"You can show off your strokes some other time," he said. "For now, let's pick up where we left off on the dance floor." Gesturing broadly, he asked, "May I have this dance?"

"Certainly," Jessica answered. Needing no prompting, she gladly fell into his embrace. Ignoring all the others now in the lake, she basked in the realization that for the evening she was Bruce Patman's girl. And she hoped it was only the beginning.

"Why have we waited so long to do this?" Bruce whispered in her ear as he circled her in the water, which came to her shoulders.

"There's a time and a place for everything, Bruce. It just wasn't our time before." Jessica's words surprised her. She didn't really believe them.

"It's our time now," Bruce said huskily. "Or it could be—if you want it." Gently pressing the back of her neck with his fingertips, he brushed his lips against hers.

"Oh, Bruce," Jessica said and sighed when their lips parted temporarily. He pulled her closer, this time for a long, lingering kiss unlike any she'd ever experienced before.

As they continued to embrace, Bruce slowly dropped his arms from her neck to her back. Too caught up in the rapture of the moment, Jessica had no idea what he was doing until she felt the cool water swirl under her bikini top and hit her breasts.

Right in front of everyone Bruce had untied her bathing suit strings! Though only her head and shoulders were visible above the water, Jessica was still shocked. Bruce was moving too far, too fast. She realized she had to retie the top without making him think she was some kind of goody-goody.

"Now, Bruce, why'd you go and do a thing like that?" she said, exaggerating a pout. Pretending to be madder than she was, she pushed him away and quickly retied the top.

Bruce smiled slyly. "What's the matter, Jess, don't you like to play big-girl games? Or are you just a tease?"

"Oh, no, Bruce. I like playing as much as you do. I just don't like to rush into things. It's more fun when you take your time. Didn't anyone ever tell you that's what girls really like?" Jessica said, moving a little farther away from him.

"So now you're playing hard to get?" Bruce said mockingly. He moved through the water, away from her.

Anxiously Jessica reached out for him, afraid he might be leaving her.

"I don't play the game by those rules," he informed her arrogantly.

"Well, maybe it's time to break the rules," Jessica said.

"Why would I want to do that?" he asked.

"For this." Swimming over to Bruce, Jessica gave him a slow, moist kiss, then murmured seductively, "Let's start all over again."

"Let's get out of here first," he said huskily. "I think we're both waterlogged."

"Sounds fine to me," she purred.

"And I know just the place we can dry off."

Their departure from the lake did not escape Elizabeth's attention. She'd been standing by the water's edge talking with some friends when she noticed her sister and Bruce embrace, then pull themselves out of the water and walk toward some trees. Uneasy about what Jessica could be getting herself into, Elizabeth turned quickly to Todd and said, "Oh, I just remembered I left something in the car. I'll be back in a sec."

"I'll come with you," Todd offered.

"N-no, I'll be fine," she said, running off before Todd had a chance to respond. As soon as she was out of his sight, Elizabeth cut a path to her left, swiftly walking in the direction where she had last seen Bruce and Jessica. Moments later, Elizabeth stood before a dense row of juniper trees that separated the lake area from the more secluded part of the Matthewses' property. Away from the festive party lights and pulsing music, it was dark and still. Elizabeth began to move through the trees, guided only by the dim glow of the moon.

It didn't take long until she heard sounds she had dreaded hearing: the sounds of two people whispering breathlessly as the leaf-covered ground crackled under the weight of their bodies. Elizabeth stopped abruptly, hoping they hadn't heard the crunching sound of her own footsteps. She was eavesdropping on a passionate moment, and it made her feel uncomfortable. Increasingly filled with distress, Elizabeth willed Jessica and Bruce to stop, hoping that her usually reckless sister would for once control her impulses. But the soft sounds continued, and Elizabeth had to make a decision.

Embarrassed or not, she resolved to approach the couple.

Deliberately coughing loudly, Elizabeth made her way through the leaves, walking slowly, hoping to give Jessica and Bruce enough time to disentangle themselves. But they refused to be warned. She was practically standing on top of them when they finally noticed her.

Jessica looked up and scowled. "God, Elizabeth, must you go sneaking up on people like Jack the

Ripper? Don't you have any respect for other people's privacy?" She was lying wrapped in Bruce's arms, and she barely turned her face from his.

Elizabeth refused to budge. "Could I see you for a minute, Jess? I've got a real important problem."

"It can wait, Liz," said a very annoyed Bruce.

"I'm talking to Jessica, not you," Elizabeth retorted. "Jess, can you come inside for a minute?"

Before Jessica had a chance to answer, Bruce raised himself on one elbow, coolly allowing his free hand to slide seductively along Jessica's right arm and come to rest on her shoulder, just above her breast.

Jessica didn't move.

"Look, honey—" Bruce started.

"I'm not your honey," Elizabeth snapped.

"Hey, whatever. Can't you see Jessica's busy? Whatever you want can wait."

"I have to talk to my sister now. Jessica?" Elizabeth's stare bored directly into her sister's eyes. "Please, Jessica," she practically pleaded.

Bruce smirked. "Go on," he said to Jessica. "I wouldn't want to hold you. Unless you want me to."

To Jessica the message was clear: Go with Elizabeth and kiss Bruce Patman goodbye. It took only a second for her to decide. "I'm not going anywhere—just now." Then, turning to Elizabeth, she added, "Look, whatever it is, I'll talk to you about it later, OK?"

Elizabeth was mortified. Jessica had never rejected her so bluntly before. It was clear that she would have needed a crowbar to pry her sister from Bruce's arms. "Forget it," Elizabeth said. There was a mixture of hurt and disgust in her voice. Then she turned and headed back to the party.

Jessica smiled. Now that she had nothing to lose, she wanted to show Bruce her strength. "Do you believe her?" she said as soon as Elizabeth was out of earshot. "Sometimes she's really off the wall."

"From the way she came stomping over here, you'd think she was your baby-sitter."

"Nah, I'm sure it has nothing to do with me." She lied easily, knowing full well it had everything to do with her. "It's probably more stuff about that guy she's madly in love with. She did say *she* had the problem. Remember?"

"Oh, yeah. You mean Todd?" Bruce asked, taken in.

"I couldn't possibly tell you," Jessica purred coyly. "After all, she is my sister, and we never betray each other's secrets, no matter what."

"But," Bruce whispered, "can you keep a secret from her?"

"What do you mean?" she asked, their faces barely inches apart.

"This," he said, and he kissed her deeply. It took her breath away, leaving her helpless in his arms.

As much as Jessica loved the way she was feeling, another part of her was disturbed. She was used to having the upper hand with boys, but already she was starting to feel out of control. She had to slow Bruce down, and now was the time to try. She blurted out the first thing that came to her mind. "Actually, I hope Liz hasn't found out the truth."

"What's that?" asked Bruce, his curiosity revived.

"That Todd's been fooling around," Jessica lied. "I can't bear to tell her. She'll be so hurt. Anyway," she added, having achieved her purpose for the moment, "we shouldn't be bothering with it. It's not our problem."

"That's for sure, baby. We don't have any problems, do we?" He kissed her again, and this time she felt herself respond with rising passion. And as Bruce's lips pressed against hers, she felt her power over him slip away.

Bruce, in control and knowing it, broke the kiss and looked deeply into her eyes. "But, baby, you'd know in a minute if we *did* have a problem."

"How?"

"By the empty space next to you."

Jessica suddenly felt insecure and vulnerable. She cuddled closer to Bruce and in her sexiest voice, with her lips tickling his ear, whispered softly, "It sure doesn't feel empty now."

He responded by turning his face to hers and kissing her hard, his arms crushing her against him, his mouth demanding what his body wanted to take.

Three

Elizabeth, rolling over, lay awake in her bed. She looked at the clock for the fortieth time. It was already after three A.M., and she hadn't slept a wink. She was not only angry at her twin, but worried, too.

About an hour after her disastrous encounter with Jessica and Bruce in the woods, Elizabeth had seen them take off in his gleaming black Porsche. She had been disgusted enough to suppress her concern and enjoy the rest of the party, but once Todd brought her home her worries returned—stronger than ever. Brooding over Jessica's whereabouts in the silence of the predawn hours was becoming almost unbearable.

On top of everything else, Elizabeth was angry

at Jessica for forcing her to lie to her mother, whom she'd run into in the upstairs hall. Lying was something Elizabeth never did, except when it came to her sister. Hoping her mother wouldn't double-check, Elizabeth had told her that Jessica was already in her bedroom. The last thing in the world she wanted to do was to sneak into Jessica's bed and pretend to be her, a routine she'd gone through more than once before. Oddly enough, her mother didn't question the lie. In fact, she didn't even ask Elizabeth about her date. She seemed preoccupied with something else, Elizabeth thought.

Just as the sun was about to make its appearance, Elizabeth heard the sound of a door close. Convinced it was Jessica, she crawled out of her bed and tiptoed through the bathroom to Jessica's adjoining room.

Jessica didn't see Elizabeth until she was nearly on top of her, and she almost woke up the entire Wakefield household with a startled gasp. "You making a habit of sneaking up on me?" Jessica fumed, trying to keep her voice down. "What gives, Liz?"

"Sorry, Jess, I didn't mean to scare you. I couldn't sleep. Where've you been?"

Jessica smiled sweetly. "I don't have to give you my itinerary, Liz, but I'd think even *you* could figure out the answer to that one."

"Bruce. You've been with him all this time?"

"Oh, yes," Jessica said blissfully. "And it was wonderful!"

"I was afraid of that," Elizabeth murmured.

"There's nothing to be afraid of," Jessica said. "Bruce is everything a girl could ever hope for."

"How could you tell? He's got you so worked up you can't even think straight."

"And what's that supposed to mean?"

"You were following him like a little puppy dog all night long. That's so unlike you, Jessica." Elizabeth lowered her voice to a whisper. "And don't think I'm not upset about the way you treated me in the woods. You've never brushed me off like that before."

"I'm sorry," Jessica said, "but you did interrupt a private moment."

"I guess I did. But for some reason I felt afraid for you, and I just couldn't control myself. I'm sorry for that," Elizabeth added truthfully.

"Afraid? I can handle myself just fine," Jessica retorted, ignoring her sister's apology.

Elizabeth was doubtful. With false lightness, she asked, "Anyway, what did you two do after the party?"

"Nothing to be ashamed of. Talk mostly." Dropping her guard for a second, Jessica confided with pleasure, "Bruce said he was angry when he lost out at being king 'cause he wanted to share the throne with me."

Elizabeth was astounded that her normally perceptive sister would fall for such an obviously phony remark. "I wouldn't believe a line like that if he took a lie detector test," she blurted.

"Oh, come on, Elizabeth. Why can't you get it into your thick skull that Bruce likes me!"

"It takes more than a few kisses to prove that."

"A lot you know. The truth is, we really have tons in common." She sighed wistfully. "Oh, I hope I'll see him again real soon."

"You mean he didn't ask you out again—after all that?"

"No," Jessica admitted, "but I'm sure he will."

"I wouldn't be," Elizabeth muttered under her breath.

"I heard that." Jessica's patience with her sister was nearing the breaking point. She flounced into the bathroom and briskly ran a brush through her long, silky hair. When Elizabeth followed her, she added, "I've had just about enough of your bad-mouthing Bruce. I don't know what you've got against him. You never tried to stop me from making a play for him before tonight."

"I never had to—he was never interested before tonight."

"Look, if there's something specific that you have to tell me about him, go ahead. Otherwise, shut up."

"He's arrogant and self-centered. He'll hurt you."

Jessica snorted. "Just what I thought. You don't have any real reasons—just your own opinion.

Sorry, Liz, but you're going to have to do better than that."

"Look how fast he dumped Lila Fowler and Heather Morgan. Even your good friend Cara Walker. Why believe *you'll* do any better? He doesn't hang on to anyone for very long."

Jessica put down her brush and faced her sister. "Liz, don't you understand? They meant nothing to him."

"How do you know?" Elizabeth pressed.

"He told me."

"And you believe him?"

"I have no reason not to. Now, are you finished?"

Elizabeth eyed her sister silently, aware that in the end Jessica would have to figure out the truth herself.

"You had your chance, Elizabeth," Jessica said angrily. "Don't you *dare* say another bad word about Bruce in front of me, or you'll regret it for eternity."

"Jess—"

"You heard me, Elizabeth! That's all!"

Before Elizabeth could recover, Jessica stormed out of the bathroom and locked the door behind her. Elizabeth stood alone in front of the vanity, her eyes brimming with tears. Despite all of the petty disagreements they'd had over the years, she couldn't remember Jessica ever going to bed angry at her. Elizabeth didn't like it one bit, especially since she was sure that the cause of their argument—that arrogant jock, Bruce Patman—was just playing another game with her unsuspecting sister. And she was almost as sure it was a game Jessica couldn't win.

Sunday morning found Elizabeth at the breakfast table, nibbling idly on a piece of toast, only half listening to her parents' conversation.

"Says here that George Fowler's expanding his plant." Alice Wakefield put down the Sunday paper as she spoke to her husband, Ned. "I'm going to call him first thing tomorrow and show him my portfolio. I could come up with some wonderful designs for him."

So that was it, Elizabeth decided distractedly. Her mother had been thinking about this Fowler project last night. That's why she'd been too preoccupied to notice Elizabeth's cover-up for Jessica.

Ned shook his head. "I don't know, honey. I hear he's already negotiating with a big design firm from San Francisco."

Alice lifted her brows in surprise and distress. "How do you know? And why didn't you tell me sooner?"

Ned's face assumed that slightly bemused expression that always came over him when they discussed his wife's career moves. "I found out from Marianna on Friday," he said offhandedly.

"It didn't seem important at the time." Marianna West was a partner in his law firm.

Alice held her breath for a moment. She was unhappy with her husband's lack of interest in her work, but she had no desire to make an issue of it on this bright, clear Sunday morning. Exhaling slowly, she changed the subject. "What were you and Marianna talking about, dear?"

Elizabeth tuned out the rest of her parents' conversation and barely heard the phone ringing in the other room. Still upset about Jessica, she could hardly even concentrate on finishing breakfast.

Alice couldn't help noticing her daughter's glum mood. "What's the matter, Liz? Did you and Todd have a fight last night?"

"Oh, no, Mom. We had a good time."

"So why the sad face?"

"It's nothing." Elizabeth attempted a halfhearted smile. "I'll be all right."

"Sure you don't want to talk about it?" Alice asked.

"I'm sure, Mom. Really, I'm fine. I just didn't sleep too well last night. Pass me the cartoons, OK? Maybe a little *Peanuts* will help."

Elizabeth was busy trying to lose herself in the comics when Jessica breezily entered the kitchen.

"Good morning, people!" She was as bubbly as a newly opened bottle of soda despite a mere three hours' sleep. "How are all of you this morning?" Without waiting for an answer, she planted a firm kiss on everyone's forehead.

Elizabeth was stunned. She couldn't remember the last time her sister had been up so early on a Sunday morning.

"What's gotten into you, Jess?" her father asked, a chuckle in his voice.

Mrs. Wakefield smiled. "Can't you tell, Ned? Obviously she had a great time at the dance."

"That's right, Mom," Jessica said, pouring herself a glass of orange juice. She leaned against the tile counter and stared dreamily off into space. "I think I'm in love," she announced at last.

"With Winston?" Her mother threw her a surprised look.

"Absolutely not! Winston's a nerd, Mom. I'm talking about someone extra special."

Elizabeth groaned, but no one heard. All eyes were on her twin.

"Who's that, dear?" Alice asked.

Jessica paused for dramatic effect. "Bruce Patman."

"The Patman boy, eh," her father noted approvingly.

"But, Jessica, what happened with Winston? I thought you went out with him last night," her mother asked a little suspiciously. She was well aware of her daughter's tendency to go after what she wanted with total disregard for other people.

"I did, but he had his eye on someone else,"

Jessica hedged, shooting a quick, hard look at Elizabeth. "We agreed to go our separate ways at Ken's party."

Elizabeth wanted to challenge the lie, but she held back at the last moment. From Jessica's behavior Elizabeth knew that her twin was no longer mad at her, and she didn't want to upset the equilibrium. At the same time, though, she wasn't sure if she could stand to sit through her starry-eyed sister's retelling of her night with Bruce. It was like listening to someone who'd been hypnotized.

" . . . and he told me we were *made* for each other. Isn't that the most romantic thing you've ever heard?" Jessica directed the question at Elizabeth, who remained unusually silent. Getting no reaction, Jessica shrugged and pranced out to the hallway to fetch her red nylon jacket from the closet. Swinging it over her shoulder, she returned to the kitchen. "Don't hold up dinner for me, OK?"

"Where are you going?" Ned asked.

"Bruce just called. He's taking me sailing on Secca Lake today. I don't know how long we'll be, but I don't want you to wait." She glanced at the wall clock. "He should be picking me up any minute now."

That was all Elizabeth needed to hear. Unwilling to watch her sister fly ecstatically out the door, Elizabeth pushed her chair away from the table.

"May I be excused? I've got a big chemistry test to study for."

"Sure, dear," her mother answered.

"Say, what's the big rush, Liz?" Jessica asked. "The test's not till Wednesday. That's practically eons from now."

"So call me a Girl Scout," Elizabeth shot back. "I believe in being prepared. A little advance studying wouldn't hurt you, either."

"I won't even dignify that remark with an answer," Jessica countered. She hurried out of the kitchen and into the foyer to wait for Bruce and his slick, shiny, black Porsche.

Four

"Liz! Liz, I've got to talk to you!"

Emily Mayer caught up with Elizabeth at her locker the following morning. Emily looked quite different from the way she appeared when performing. The petite drummer was dressed for school in a plain navy blue skirt and sweater, her wavy hair tied back neatly. "Liz, it's happening," she said excitedly. "It's really happening!"

"Slow down, Emily. What are you talking about?"

"The Droids. We're going to the top of the charts!"

It took Elizabeth a second to remember. "You mean, that guy . . . what's his name?"

"Tony." Emily nodded excitedly. "He's everything he says he is, Liz. Guy even found pictures of him with some of his other bands in some back issues of *Music Madness*. I always thought it was dumb of Guy to save those magazines, but now I'm glad he did. Oh, Liz, Tony has such great plans for us."

"So when's the first record coming out?"

"Come on, we're not ready for that yet. Tony's planning to book us into some local clubs first and maybe get us some dates around the state during Christmas vacation. With a little luck and a lot of hard work, he says we may be good enough to break into L.A. clubs by next summer. But he's not promising anything. Not yet, anyway, though he did say he's going to bring around lots of record-producer friends of his to meet us as soon as we sound a little tighter."

Elizabeth smiled warmly at Emily. She took her music very seriously, and she deserved to have good things happen. "I'm so happy for you, Emily," Elizabeth bubbled. "I bet the others are just losing their minds with excitement!"

"You bet they're excited—and tired," Emily was saying as the first bell for the next class rang. The two of them began walking to class. "We were up half the night practicing."

"Seems the only thing you're missing is some publicity."

"Do you have anything in mind?"

"Yes. I'd like to chart your progress in a running series of stories in *The Oracle*. I'll have to get the go-ahead from Penny, the editor, but I know she'll love the idea. I'll begin with how you met Tony and what your plans are. Then I'll follow you from your first club date all the way to your number-one hit record."

Emily was overjoyed. "That's fantastic. Oh, Liz, you don't know how much all this means to me."

"I think I do, Emily. Being a rock star is just a fantasy for most kids, but you're actually going to live it!"

"Unfortunately I still have to live out the role of a student, too." Groaning, Emily opened the door to their chemistry class. "Reality, for the moment, is big bad Bob Russo."

They exchanged knowing glances. Chemistry was Elizabeth's hardest subject this year, and Bob Russo was the reason. A no-nonsense man, Russo was the type of teacher who demanded excellence from all his students—and usually got it. In truth, most of the kids felt he deserved their attention. He really cared what his students learned, and he insisted that they not disappoint him, or themselves. Even Jessica, who did very little studying but still got good grades in most classes, found it necessary to study for Russo's chemistry class.

When the late bell rang, Elizabeth was surprised to find her sister's chair empty as she took her own seat by the window of the second-story chemistry lab. She and Jessica had driven to school together, so she knew Jessica was around some-place. But where?

A glance out the window answered Elizabeth's question. She saw a couple kissing brazenly—and passionately—on the far end of the campus lawn. Jessica and Bruce. They were locked in an embrace so tight it seemed to Elizabeth that it would take at least half of Sweet Valley's football team to tear them apart.

Jessica ran her fingers through Bruce's dark, wavy hair, delighting in its soft, silky feel. Bruce answered her by kissing her more and more deeply, exciting every nerve ending in her body. Jessica pulled herself even closer, rubbing her other hand in small circles at the nape of Bruce's neck.

The faint sound of the late bell distracted the couple as they parted to catch their breath.

"Oh, no, Bruce, we're late! We've got to go!" Jessica quickly picked up the books she'd strewn across the grass earlier.

Bruce chuckled and placed a hand on Jessica's shoulder to keep her in place. "What's the rush, baby? We were just getting started."

Jessica couldn't look him in the face. She wanted desperately to be with him, but she didn't relish paying the price later with the stern chemistry teacher. "I want to stay, Bruce. You know that.

But I've got to get to Russo's class. He'll kill me if I cut it."

"You mean to tell me my girl's more interested in Mr. Chemistry than in me? What about *our* chemistry? I thought I knew you better, Jess."

She sighed. "Oh, Bruce, you know how I feel about us." Then, her fingers lightly caressing the back of his neck, she continued. "But you know how he is about giving out detentions, and if I have to stay after school, I won't be able to watch you practice tennis. You wouldn't like that, Bruce, would you?"

"I see your point, but . . . Hey, not to worry, sweet thing." Reaching into the back pocket of his corduroy pants, Bruce pulled out a pad. "Even Russo can't refuse to accept this." Bruce scribbled something on the top sheet, ripped it off, and handed it to Jessica.

"A note from the nurse's office!" Jessica glowed, relieved she didn't have to make a choice she had no desire to make.

Bruce traced the outline of her mouth with his fingertip. "The results of my examination show you need some mouth-to-mouth resuscitation."

Jessica moved closer. "I'd say your diagnosis is right on the mark, Dr. Patman. Shall we begin the treatments?" Raising her face to his, Jessica entwined herself around her beloved boyfriend.

Five

The following afternoon Elizabeth rushed home from school as soon as classes ended. During her last-period gym class, as she was playing tennis with her best friend, Enid, she'd had an idea for a short story. Elizabeth loved the special, excited feeling that came over her whenever inspiration struck, but she knew the idea would fade unless she got her thoughts on paper as soon as possible. She hoped to finish a rough outline before the day was through.

No one else was home, and the solitude provided Elizabeth with the atmosphere she needed to concentrate. Retreating to her favorite over-stuffed chair in the living room, she opened her spiral notebook and began to put her thoughts down on paper. The story was about a girl who kept making the wrong decisions in love.

A short while later Elizabeth became aware of a knocking sound. At first it was so timid that she thought it was a tree limb banging softly against the side of the house. But the knock became more persistent, and Elizabeth realized someone was at the front door. Reluctantly she put aside her notebook to answer it. On the other side of the threshold stood Robin Wilson.

"Hi, Liz, is Jessica here?" she asked.

"No," said Elizabeth. "She's at cheerleading practice. But I expect her back soon. Tonight's her night to make dinner."

Robin looked confused. "I checked at cheerleading practice. She wasn't there. We were going to spend the afternoon together, but she never showed up. Gee, I wonder where she could be."

"I think I know," Elizabeth said, realizing she'd better start thinking about what *she'd* like to make for dinner. "I'll bet anything she's out with Bruce Patman."

"Oh." Robin lowered her head, trying to hide her disappointment.

You've done it again, Jessica, Elizabeth thought. Although Elizabeth didn't know Robin that well, she felt sorry for the pudgy girl standing before her. All she wanted was to be Jessica's friend, even though all Jessica seemed to want was to take advantage of Robin's good nature. Elizabeth decided to put her story on hold and invite Robin inside.

"I'm sorry Jessica's not here," she said once they were seated. "You should tell her she can't just change plans on you like this."

"Oh, that's OK," Robin said quickly. "I'm sure she didn't mean it. I know *I'd* probably forget to meet a girlfriend if Bruce Patman asked me out—although the chances of that are less than zero." Flashing an embarrassed grin, she pointed to her ample midsection. "But it doesn't bother me. Jessica thinks I've already got a guy. At least that's what she tells me. That's why we were getting together today. To buy me some new clothes. Then we were coming back here to do experiments."

"For chemistry class?"

"No, to see if we could make my face sexier through science." She smiled, then sighed wistfully. "I guess it'll just have to wait till tomorrow."

Elizabeth was sure Jessica wouldn't pay any attention to Robin as long as Bruce was in the picture, but curiosity about the new boy in Robin's life overshadowed any inclination she might have had to express her doubt.

"You don't have to tell me," she began, "but who's the guy with the crush on you?"

Robin blushed as she whispered, "Winston Egbert."

"You're kidding!" Elizabeth exclaimed. She couldn't believe Winston had recovered so quickly from his heartbreak over Jessica. After all, he'd been crazy about her ever since fifth grade.

"Believe me, I understand your surprise," Robin said, grinning. "I couldn't believe it myself when Jessica told me he'd had a thing for me ever since I came to Sweet Valley. Imagine, a popular guy like Winston wanting a girl like me. He took me to Ken's party last Saturday, and we had a great time. At least I did," she added hastily.

Elizabeth was dumbstruck. "Yeah, I saw you together," she managed to say, trying to hide her shock at Jessica's latest little bit of manipulation. She was convinced Jessica had put Robin and Winston together to get them both out of her hair at the same time. Elizabeth also felt that Robin deserved to know the truth instead of being duped into believing a fantasy of Jessica's creation. "Robin, it's hard to tell you this, but Win's been interested in my sister for quite some time. I don't know if he's really ready to get involved with someone else."

A momentary look of concern crossed Robin's face as Elizabeth spoke, but it was followed quickly by a sigh of relief. "Don't worry, Liz, I know all about Jessica and Winston. She told me there was never anything much to it. They're just friends."

Elizabeth shook her head slightly. "I don't think you heard what I said. It's possible that Win isn't ready for you—or for that matter, anybody."

"But Jessica told me—"

"She's not right all the time. Look, I'm sure Win thinks you're nice. I just don't want you to get your hopes up. I know Winston's really hung up on Jess. The last thing you want is a boy on the rebound."

"No," Robin hedged. "You're wrong, Liz."

"You mean you think he's definitely over Jess?" Elizabeth asked.

"No," said Robin, smiling. "I mean I'd definitely take him on the rebound." They both laughed.

"In that case, I hope I'm wrong for your sake," Elizabeth said. She was beginning to like Robin. "By the way, got any plans for Saturday night?"

"Not yet."

"Well, if nothing comes up, why don't you join Todd and me? We're going to a club down in Sand Pines to see The Droids."

"I don't know. I don't want to tag along on your date."

"It's not an actual 'date' date. I'm writing an article for *The Oracle* on The Droids, so it's more like an assignment for me. I think it might be a good place for you to meet some guys. You don't have to give me an answer now, but promise me you'll consider it, OK?"

Robin thought a moment before answering. "OK," she said. Then she got up and headed for the door. "I'd better be getting home now. You'll tell Jessica I stopped by, won't you?"

"Don't worry," Elizabeth said with a gleam in her eye. "You can be sure I'll tell her."

Elizabeth was taking that night's dinner of roast chicken out of the oven when Jessica showed up. Following the aroma into the kitchen, Jessica purred, "Umm, something smells good."

"I gather you're going to grace us with your presence tonight?"

"Of course. I live here. Oh, and thanks for making dinner tonight. I promise I'll make it up to you sometime."

"With you, 'sometime' could be around the year 2000. I won't hold my breath," Elizabeth retorted.

"Look, I'm really sorry I was late. I . . . um . . . had something important to do."

"I know. Something called Bruce Patman."

Jessica looked genuinely surprised. "You and your intuition."

"Actually, Robin stopped by earlier. She said you and she were supposed to get together this afternoon."

"Was that today?" Jessica feigned forgetfulness. "I must have mixed up the dates."

"You really disappointed her," Elizabeth chided.

"She'll get over it." Jessica shrugged, unconcerned. "It was just a trip to the mall."

"I have a feeling it was more than 'just a trip' to

her. The least you could have done was told her you couldn't make it."

"Oh, she'll understand. We can do her makeover anytime—though I do admit, the sooner the better. Honestly, Liz, I simply forgot. Bruce came up to me right after the last bell and took me for a ride up Valley Crest Highway. It was fantastic."

"How fantastic can a ride on the highway be, Jessica?" Elizabeth asked with distaste.

"We talked about what great times we're going to have together." Jessica's face took on that faraway, dreamy look that came over her whenever the subject turned to Bruce.

"What kind of 'great times'?" Elizabeth pressed.

"Oh, for starters, right after I grab a bite I'm going over to Bruce's to show him he's not the only good tennis player in Sweet Valley. Don't wait up for me, either. It'll probably be a late night."

"Gee, Jess, I thought you'd be around tonight to go over our notes for tomorrow's chemistry test."

"You still worried about that?"

"Aren't you? You're barely getting by as it is."

"But I always pull through, don't I?"

A half hour later Jessica stood on the Patmans' tennis court. Cut into the hill right below the stately Patman mansion, the court overlooked

Sweet Valley, and Jessica could see her own house near the bottom of the slope. Swinging her racket lightly, she turned to Bruce as he approached from the house. "I love it up here. The view is gorgeous."

Bruce's eyes were focused on Jessica's legs, long and tanned beneath her short tennis whites. "I like the view, too," he told her. "Ready to play?"

"Let's volley first."

Bruce opened a can of balls and bounced one in the air with his racket. "I can't think of a better way to spend the evening."

"Me, either—though my sister thinks I should be studying."

"Doesn't she believe in having fun?"

"Oh, she's worried about this big test we're having tomorrow. But what she doesn't know is that I have a secret weapon."

"What's that, baby?"

"Not what. Who. Emily Mayer. She sits next to me, and she's practically Albert Einstein at chemistry. And her handwriting is neat—and large, if you get my point."

Bruce winked knowingly, then positioned himself at the far end of the court. "I think it's time I got your mind off chemistry," he said, getting ready to serve. "Here goes."

He smashed the ball into Jessica's court, using the same competitive, game-strength force he would have with any opponent. Jessica returned the serve with a clean, hard backhand down the line—much to Bruce's surprise. He was not amused. "Hey, what's the idea?" he grumbled.

"Just brushing up on my game, Bruce," Jessica said, pleased with her shot. Bruce was a very strong player, but she was confident she could hold her own against him.

She couldn't hear what Bruce muttered under his breath, but she could see that the smile was now gone from his face. Again he smashed the ball across the court—and again Jessica's natural reaction was to hit it back. Perfectly.

"Who do you think you are, Chris Evert Lloyd?" Bruce yelled across the net. It was clear he didn't mean it as a compliment. "Your serve." Angrily he threw her a ball.

Jessica bounced the ball a few times. She didn't like the way Bruce was glaring at her, as if she'd committed a cardinal sin by playing her best. Obviously he didn't like to lose.

Neither did she, but the more she considered the anger in Bruce's icy blue eyes, the more she began to reconsider her options. She was clearly on top of her game this evening, but maybe that wasn't such a good thing. Bruce didn't appear to appreciate her skill, and it was obvious he would be angry at her if she ended up winning. Carrying that logic one step further, she concluded he'd probably decide not to play with her anymore. He might even decide she was too aggressive off the court as well and dump her altogether.

That was a possibility Jessica couldn't bear. So she did the only thing she could to protect herself. For the first time in her life, she actually tried to lose at something.

During the rest of the match, she handled her racket as if she'd developed a sudden case of tennis elbow. Bruce won the set easily, 6-love.

Jessica got the first clue that she'd played it the right way when Bruce jumped the net after the set was over. Smiling now, he dropped his racket and wrapped her in a big bear hug. "To the victor go the spoils," he announced with pleasure, "and I'm taking my reward right now." Lowering his head, he kissed her hard on the lips, sending a thrilling shiver down her spine.

He really loves me, Jessica thought wildly, enjoying the comforting sensation of being enveloped in his arms. *And if it makes him happy to have a girl who wants what he wants, then that's the kind of girl I'll be.*

In Max Dellon's basement, near the Sweet Valley shopping district on the other side of town, Emily Mayer sat fretfully over her drum set. She was trying to work out the beat to the new song Guy Chesney had written for that weekend. Guy was clearly annoyed at his drummer. "What's your problem, Mayer?"

Emily pounded her bass drum in frustration. "Give me a break, Guy. You just handed me this sheet an hour ago. I'm doing the best I can."

"That may not be good enough."

"What's that supposed to mean?" Dana Larson cut in. "The girl said she's trying her best."

"Look, Dana," Guy snapped, directing his comments to the attractive lead singer. "We're getting a shot at the big time now. Saturday night's our first chance to prove ourselves, and we can't afford to make any mistakes. If Emily can't cut it, maybe we should find a new drummer."

"Maybe what we need is a new keyboard player," Dana countered pointedly. "Jeez, Guy, who do you think you are, talking like that? We're a group. We stick together. All of us."

Max looked up from his guitar and shook his head. "You guys are something." He chuckled. "Getting all worked up over some two-bit gig. What's the big deal?"

"If you don't know, maybe we'd better think about replacing you, too," Guy snarled.

"Hey, lighten up," Max drawled. "We've never had any hassles like this before."

"All we've played are school dances and parties," Guy pointed out. "Small-time stuff. When we go on on Saturday night, we've got to be cooking. And we won't unless certain people in this band

57

get their act together!'' He shot another warning look at Emily.

"I'm working on it, Guy," Emily said through clenched teeth.

Dana had heard enough. "Look, Guy, I know you're under a lot of pressure to make this work. But there's no need to get so upset. We're all under pressure. Apologize to Emily and tell her you didn't mean what you said."

"Yeah," added Dan Scott, the bass guitar player, "we don't have all night."

Guy scratched his neck and thought for a long time. "I guess Dana's right, Emily," he said finally. "I'm letting this gig get to me. Sorry I jumped all over you. Friends?"

"Friends," she answered weakly, forcing a smile. "Let's try it again from the top, OK?"

"You heard the girl," Guy addressed the rest of the group. "Let's hit it. One, two, three, four!"

All tension faded as the music took over. Each run-through sounded better than the last, and soon even Guy was happy with their progress. By the end of the night, he was convinced they'd bring down the house that weekend.

But Emily didn't forget his earlier warning, though she secretly believed his frustration and anger were caused more by his unreturned affection for Dana than anything to do with the band. He'd never said as much to Emily, but she was sure she hadn't misread the look on Guy's face every time the group's singer smiled at him. What-ever the source of Guy's problems, though, Emily was anxious not to push her luck. After the group decided to call it a night, she went home and practiced every song in The Droids' repertoire.

It was only as she was getting undressed for bed that she remembered Russo's test. Slipping under the covers, an exhausted Emily opened her chemistry book. But ten minutes later, the lights still on and the textbook uselessly on the floor where it had fallen, she was sound asleep.

Six

"I don't believe it. I just don't believe it!" Jessica wiped a hand across her tear-streaked face, then threw herself into Bruce's arms. It was lunchtime on Friday, and the couple was sitting under one of the many white oak trees that graced the Sweet Valley High campus.

Bruce couldn't imagine what had happened, but he liked playing the role of Jessica's savior. Sure that he knew exactly what she really wanted, he began to caress and stroke her back gently. Nibbling at her ear, he whispered, "Hey, I'm not going to let anything upset my baby. What's wrong, Jess?"

Jessica pulled away just enough to look directly into Bruce's concerned blue eyes. "That idiot Mr.

Russo had the nerve to give me an F on my chemistry test," she cried.

Bruce stroked her cheeks tenderly. "No more tears, babe. It's only a dumb test."

"It's more than that. You don't understand, Bruce. I was just getting by before this, and now I might fail the whole semester!"

"Calm down, Jess. Maybe this will help." Bruce gave her a deep, lingering kiss.

"That was nice, Bruce," Jessica said when they parted. "Unfortunately it doesn't solve my problem."

"But there's a solution to every problem. Tell me what happened."

"Remember my secret weapon, Emily Mayer? She let me down. This time she failed the test, too."

"So next time cheat off someone else's paper."

"I have a feeling if I switch seats now, Russo will get suspicious." Jessica anxiously picked at the grass by her side. "Bruce, what am I going to do?"

He clasped her hands in his. "First of all, you've got to see that flunking chemistry isn't the end of the world. What are you ever going to use it for, anyway?"

"I haven't the foggiest idea. But if I flunk, I'm off the cheerleading squad. And *that* I care about."

"A bunch of silly-looking girls jumping up and down and yelling in front of a lot of people?"

Bruce patted Jessica's head as if she were a little girl. "You care about the strangest things."

Jessica didn't like his tone, but she didn't want to risk upsetting him by making an issue of it. So she quickly switched gears, pretending she didn't care about the squad. "Well, I have to admit it's been getting a little boring lately. And I did miss a few practices this week. But even so, it would be humiliating to be kicked off the squad."

"Well, you've come to the right person," Bruce declared.

Jessica looked up at him with hope. She knew Bruce would come to her rescue. "What do you mean?" she asked.

"I should have told you the other night that you shouldn't count on unreliable people like Emily. I've got a foolproof way for you to get an A in chemistry."

"Bruce!" Jessica's eyes widened expectantly. "Tell me!"

Taking his time, enjoying the suspense, Bruce stretched out his legs and leaned against the oak. "It's simple." He smiled confidently. "I know where Russo keeps his tests."

Jessica threw her arms around Bruce's neck. "And you'll get them for me!"

Bruce pulled back abruptly, willing to play the hero only to a point. "No way. *My* days of messing with that man are over. But I'll tell you how to get them without being caught."

Jessica bit her lower lip. She would have preferred it if Bruce simply handed her the tests, but she was in no position to argue. "Sure, Bruce. Tell me where they are."

"Later," he whispered, moving closer. "First we've got to take care of business." Bruce wrapped his arms around Jessica, and together they fell onto the soft grass, exchanging kisses with a frantic urgency.

On the other side of the campus, Elizabeth carried her lunch tray to the outdoor eating area, scanning the rows of tables for an empty seat. She found one next to Winston, who sat staring down at a book, though he looked as if he hadn't the faintest idea what he was reading. "Uh, mind if I take a seat?" Elizabeth asked.

Taking a quick glance at her, Winston smiled ecstatically, not daring to believe that his fantasy had come true. The smile faded quickly, however, when he realized which Wakefield twin it was. "Oh, hi, Liz," he said glumly. "The seat's yours if you want it."

"That's not the friendliest offer I've had all day, but I'll take it." She placed her tray on the table. "What are you reading?"

Winston put down the book. "You've got me. Something to do with economics." He shrugged. "I didn't mean to sound unfriendly, Liz. I was just thinking. I'd probably be better off if I gave it all up—school, girls, my car—and joined the nearest monastery.''

Elizabeth put an arm around his shoulder. "I never thought of you as the type to get the calling. You sure about this?''

"Nah," he admitted, "but it would make life a lot simpler."

"Why do I have the feeling this has to do with girls? Say one girl in particular?"

Winston looked at her sadly. "Am I that transparent?''

Elizabeth smiled. "Not at all, Win," she lied gently. "I just happen to be her sister. You want to talk?"

Winston drummed his fingers on the table for a second or two, then let out a deep sigh. "You're right. It's Jessica."

"I know you're upset about the way she's been treating you. You have every right to be, as far as I'm concerned."

"That's not all that's bothering me, Liz. I know Jessica doesn't care for me as much as I'd like, and I can live with that for now. What's getting to me is that she's wasting her time and affection on that jerk Patman."

Elizabeth nodded. "I've been trying to tell her the same thing for days. Until now we've always been able to talk out our differences, but for the first time in our lives, she's shut me out completely.

I mean, I have to admit I *have* been pretty critical of their relationship, but Bruce is like a god to her, and I can't stand it! She considers it a cardinal sin if I say *anything* critical about him. All I have to do is say one negative word about him, and she walks away in a huff."

"It sounds like she's really fallen for him hard."

"That's putting it mildly, Win. You wouldn't believe the change in her. In one week she's turned into a new person—Bruce's slave. Yesterday, for instance, she skipped cheerleading practice to take Bruce's tennis outfits to the dry cleaners. Then she went to the Record House to buy some cassettes Bruce wanted—with her own money, no less. Can you imagine the old Jessica doing that?"

Winston sighed. "We can't let her go on like this."

"I can't stop her." Sadly Elizabeth looked down at the tuna salad she'd barely touched. Jessica's love life was ruining her appetite more than her own ever had, she mused.

"But there's got to be something we can do!" Winston insisted.

Elizabeth thrust a forkful of salad into her mouth. It tasted like wet cotton. "Look, I think we both need to change the subject. Got any plans for tomorrow night?"

Winston shook his head. "Besides a hot date with my Atari? No, nothing doing."

"The Droids are playing their first big-time gig

tomorrow night. Want to come along with Todd and me?"

"The Droids? How come I haven't heard about this?"

"They've been quiet about it because they don't want the audience full of kids from Sweet Valley. They want to see how their stuff'll go over with a bunch of strangers."

"I'd go see them wherever they're playing."

"Yeah. Me, too," Elizabeth agreed, but the next moment she sucked in her breath. "Win, listen, I just remembered something. Please don't get the wrong idea, but I also asked Robin Wilson to come along." She looked down at her plate hesitantly.

"Not you, too!" Winston exclaimed. "What's with you Wakefield girls? Why the big push to get me and Robin together?"

"I didn't mean it that way. I told you, I forgot for a second that I'd asked her. I just thought that since you didn't have any plans, you might want to go with Todd and me."

Winston studied Elizabeth affectionately. "That was nice of you. But Robin . . . well, she's OK. We really don't have much in common, though. I get nervous around people who eat all the time."

"You don't have to feel like it's a date. There'll probably be lots of new faces at the club. And you can use a change of atmosphere. What do you say?"

"I don't have to stick with Robin?"

"You're riding in the same car together, that's all. You're free to do whatever you want after that."

"In that case, what time are you picking me up?"

Seven

Late Saturday afternoon Elizabeth stepped out of the shower and began to get ready for her night out. She dried off, put on her bathrobe, then, after wiping off the steam-covered mirror, she ran a wide-toothed comb through her long, thick hair as she tried to figure out what to wear. Mentally rejecting most of her wardrobe, she finally decided to ask Jessica if she could borrow one of her wilder, flashier outfits. "You can't go to a rock club looking like your own grandmother," she muttered to her reflection.

She hoped Jessica wouldn't give her a hard time. At least they were talking again. Trying to keep the lines of communication open between them, Elizabeth had stopped criticizing Bruce. She figured that as long as she kept him out of the conversation, her relationship with Jessica stood a good chance of returning to normal. She also hoped it would increase the chances of Jessica's confiding in her, should she need to.

As Elizabeth finished blow-drying her hair, she heard a knock on the bathroom door. "Come in," she called out.

Jessica, smiling and balancing an armload of packages from her afternoon shopping spree, stood in the doorway. "Come take a look at what I bought," she squealed excitedly. "I found the most heavenly dresses at The Boston Shop."

"You went *where?*" Elizabeth couldn't believe her ears. The twins had always avoided that exclusive women's store, a place where a lot of snobby types did their shopping. Filled with curiosity, Elizabeth followed Jessica into her room. "You swore you'd never set foot in that place."

"That was before," Jessica said, opening up one of the packages.

Elizabeth didn't have to ask "before what?" "Let me see what you got," she said resignedly.

Triumphantly Jessica pulled a brown wool blazer and matching skirt out of one bag and two oxford shirts from another. The look was tasteful, classic, and rich—yet very unlike Jessica. "Aren't these the most elegant clothes you've ever seen?"

Elizabeth looked at her sister in total bewilderment. "Weren't you the one who always said that people who dress preppy have no originality?"

"That was silly of me, wasn't it?" Jessica threw the blazer over her shoulders and smiled. "Bruce thinks this is a smart look, especially for a girl with long legs like mine. He's taking me to the country club for dinner." She put the jacket on her bed and held the two shirts against it. "Which do you think looks better? The beige or the pink?"

Elizabeth longed to ask her sister why she was letting Bruce run her life, but she had the distinct feeling that Jessica wouldn't understand what she was talking about, anyway. Without further comment on her sister's changed wardrobe, Elizabeth chose the pink blouse. "Speaking of clothes," she added, "I was wondering if I could borrow your black and white miniskirt tonight."

"You can keep it forever," Jessica said airily. "I'll never need it. Bruce can't stand New Wave clothes. He says they look cheap. But don't get me wrong, that skirt would look cute on you with a black body suit."

"Yeah, thanks," Elizabeth responded dryly. She could only guess at what other changes Bruce would force on her sister. Knowing she was on the brink of saying something about Bruce, she decided to excuse herself from Jessica's room quickly. "Todd's picking me up soon, so I'd better get dressed. Have a good time tonight."

"Don't worry." Jessica winked suggestively as her sister stood in the doorway. "Bruce and I always do."

The light fog rolling in from the Pacific made the visibility on the coast road poor, and Todd almost drove past the Seaside Express, the club where The Droids were playing. "Whoa, Todd," Winston shouted from the backseat of Todd's Datsun. "There's the place."

"This is it?" Todd exclaimed as he pulled into the dirt-covered drive. Before them stood a low, wood-shingled building that had definitely seen better days. No more than a dozen cars were parked in the lot.

"There's the sign: Sand Pines," Winston noted.

"Your eyes must be better than mine," Todd said, shaking his head in disbelief. "I don't know how you even saw it. It looks like no one's been near it for decades."

He turned to Elizabeth. "You sure The Droids are playing here? The place looks deserted."

"Sure, see the sign in the window? This is it. Maybe the fog's keeping people away."

"Maybe not. It's still early, isn't it?" Winston's voice had an almost desperate sound to it. If no one else showed up, he knew he'd have to spend the rest of the evening with Robin.

"It's *not* that early," Todd said flatly. "I don't

know about you, but I wouldn't mind just staying for a few numbers, then heading back to Sweet Valley. I don't like the looks of this place."

"We can't leave that quickly, Todd," Elizabeth stated firmly. "I've got to see their act. Besides, we're here already—and it doesn't look all that bad to me!"

"I don't want to leave," said Robin, looking hopefully at Winston.

Todd shrugged. "I suppose we'll survive." He reached over and opened the door on Elizabeth's side. "Shall we?"

On the way up the graveled path to the club's entrance, Todd paused to admire a motorcycle parked off to the side. "This Virago's a beaut, don't you think, Liz?"

Elizabeth frowned. "It's just a pile of metal. I don't think I'll ever understand what you see in these machines."

"Just wait, Liz. When I get my bike, you'll see how much fun they are."

Inside, the club's dim lighting helped mask the cheap paneled walls marred by scratches and dents.

Todd took Elizabeth by the arm protectively. "Let's find seats."

Only a few of the small black tables and chairs were occupied. Looking around, Elizabeth recognized Tony Conover, The Droids' new manager, seated alone near the back of the room, staring intently at the small stage, where the group was already performing. He seemed to be the only one paying attention. The dance floor was empty. Only a handful of people were listening to the music. The rest were huddled together in a corner, nursing drinks and cigarettes, talking very loudly. *They must be club regulars*, Elizabeth thought.

Elizabeth and Todd took seats at one of the vacant tables near the dance floor while Winston and Robin checked out the room from the entrance. Winston, realizing this was not the night he was going to meet the girl of his dreams, reluctantly followed his friends to the table, with Robin happily accompanying him. The group ordered a round of sodas, and Elizabeth took out her notebook to begin jotting down her impressions of the place.

After taking a close look around, she decided to leave a description of the club out of her article. It was pretty seedy. *If this is the first rung on the ladder to success*, she thought, *The Droids have a very long way to go.*

If the band members were disappointed by the surroundings, it was impossible for Elizabeth to tell. They were totally involved with their music. It was clear they'd all practiced hard for this engagement; they sounded more together now than ever. They looked more professional, too. Dana had honed her style so that she now strutted around like a self-confident star. She and Emily had also invested in eye-catching red jumpsuits, and the visual effect was powerful. Max, Dan, and Guy had coordinated their outfits and looked like a trio of alluring tough guys.

After the second song, Elizabeth put away her notebook and coaxed Todd onto the dance floor. It didn't matter to them that they were the only ones dancing, and when Elizabeth looked up at the group and got a grateful wink and smile from Emily, she knew her gesture was appreciated. Winston and Robin remained at the table, neither one saying a word.

Robin was very disappointed. Despite what Elizabeth had told her, she had hoped this would be a night to remember. Jessica had taken Robin shopping with her that afternoon, and all Jessica had talked about was how much Winston was looking forward to this date. She'd assured Robin that this was an opportunity not to be wasted. She'd even insisted on taking Robin to the store in the mall that specialized in large sizes and had personally picked the peach tunic top Robin was wearing. "Winston loves this color," Jessica had told her. Even though it wasn't very flattering to her figure, Robin had snatched the garment on the spot.

But from the moment she'd stepped into Todd's car, Robin could tell the night wasn't going to live up to her expectations. Winston had been friendly when he greeted her, but when she had tried to move closer to him on the seat, he had squirmed away uncomfortably. He'd barely spoken to her at all during the forty-five minute ride, directing most of his comments to the front seat. Far from the easygoing, talkative person she had encountered at the dance, Winston had appeared preoccupied and not at all interested in being with her. Now, sitting next to her at the table, he seemed even more distant and uncomfortable. Robin began to regret that she'd agreed to come. She kept glancing at her watch, hoping the night would end as soon as possible. She was grateful when Elizabeth and Todd said they wanted to leave after the first set. Her torture would soon be over.

By the time they got back on the coast highway, the fog had lifted, revealing a clear, star-filled sky. The group was quiet, as the evening had been a disappointment for all of them. Elizabeth passed the time gazing out at the shoreline. She found the scenery hauntingly beautiful and thought that someday she'd like to sit by the sea and write a story.

About five miles from the turnoff for Sweet Valley, Elizabeth noticed a black Porsche parked along one of the side roads leading to the water. When she realized who it belong to, she let out a gasp. Not that there was only one black Porsche in the whole world, but the license plate 1BRUCE1 gave away its owner's identity. It was Bruce Patman's.

So much for a night at the country club.

Elizabeth didn't want to think about what Bruce

and her sister were doing on that dark, deserted path. She wanted to forget she'd seen the car.

But Robin wouldn't let her. "Hey, isn't that Bruce Patman's car?" she cried as they passed the gleaming vehicle. "I wonder what it's doing down here. He and Jessica were going out tonight, weren't they, Liz?"

"Yes, Robin."

"They make a really super-looking couple, don't you think?" Robin prattled. "But everyone in school seems down on them. I wonder why."

"Some things aren't worth wondering about," Winston muttered.

"Well, I'm really happy for Jessica. She told me she's in love with Bruce. I think that's so romantic. She's so beautiful, and he's gorgeous. They deserve each other, I'd say."

"I'd say you've said enough," Winston grumbled. "Look, Todd, would you mind taking me home first? I'm done in."

Robin sank as deeply into the seat as she could. *Me and my big mouth*, she berated herself. She was sure she'd just thrown any chance she might have had with Winston right out the window.

A short while later, after dropping off Winston and Robin, Todd pulled up in front of Elizabeth's house. They exchanged a kiss—it was warm and loving, and Elizabeth found it comforting. *Todd always seems to know what I need*, she told herself. Then she fell into the crook of Todd's arm. "I'm glad you understand about tonight. I had no idea the place was such a dive."

"I didn't mind, really. I just feel sorry for The Droids. Their first big date—and it's a bust."

"Yeah, a disappointing night for a lot of people."

"Like our friends in the backseat?"

Elizabeth nodded. "Poor Win. I don't ever remember seeing him so quiet. Maybe I shouldn't have talked him into coming."

"Nah, even a bad night out is better than a lonely night at home. Though, if you ask me, he didn't even give Robin a chance."

"Win made it very clear to me that he wasn't interested in her. I invited him along because I thought it'd help him take his mind off Jessica."

Todd sighed. "It figures she's at the bottom of this. That girl causes more trouble than anyone I've ever known."

"Oh, it's not her fault she doesn't love him. He's had a thing for her for way too long."

"He's wasting his time."

"I know. But he can't get her out of his system." She sighed. "Funny, it sounds exactly like Jessica's feelings about Bruce."

"But Jessica's doing something about her feelings. Ask anybody." Elizabeth shot him a questioning look, and Todd turned away quickly. He felt he'd said more than he wanted to and hoped she would change the subject.

But there was no way she could let that remark

slip by. "Just what do you mean by that, Todd?" she demanded. He remained silent, but Elizabeth was persistent. "You're hiding something from me, aren't you?" She pulled away from him and directed her piercing stare at him.

Todd gave in under her gaze. "I didn't want to tell you," he began, "but your sister is getting quite a reputation around school. Bruce has been making it very clear that he's getting everything he wants out of her. And whenever he wants it, too."

Elizabeth put her hands to her ears. "I don't believe it, Todd. Jessica would never be like that!"

Todd considered this. "Bruce could be exaggerating," he said after a pause. "I wouldn't put it past him."

"Yes, that's it," Elizabeth agreed eagerly. "He *must* be exaggerating. That's so rotten! Jessica would die if she knew she was being talked about like that."

"I don't know, Liz. She's so starry-eyed over him, I don't think she'd care."

"Oh, that Bruce Patman. If I didn't hate him before, I certainly do now. He's turned her into a completely different person. I mean, when she's not out with him, she's practically a hermit. Whenever I ask her to come someplace with me, she says she has to stay home in case Bruce calls. 'What if I miss him?' she asked me the other night. Do you believe that? Can you imagine *my sister* waiting for a boy to call?"

"Not the Jessica I know and hate."

Elizabeth ignored his last remark. "And then finally he did call—just to tell her he'd see her tonight. Todd, you should have seen the look on her face. It was as if someone had just crowned her Miss America. She looked so—so satisfied. And for what? A lousy phone call!"

"Well, wait a second, Liz. She really cares about the guy. Of course she's going to be happy to see him. Not *everything* Jessica does or feels for him is horrible!" Todd fondly cupped Elizabeth's chin in his hand. "Don't you feel good when I call?"

Gently Elizabeth gave Todd a soft kiss then thoughtfully responded, "Of course I do, and you're right. I should try to be more understanding. It's just that she's getting so carried away."

"Yes, well, she's got it bad for him."

Elizabeth leaned back in her seat dejectedly. "I tell you, Todd, he's like an evil wizard, out to twist her into anything he wants. And the worst part is, she's letting him. I wish there were something I could do to stop her."

"You've already tried—and look where it's gotten you."

"I know." She sighed. "But you don't know how awful it is to watch your sister go through all

79

this and not be able to do a thing about it. She's heading for a disaster. I can feel it, and if I don't find a way to show her what's really happening, I'm afraid I'll lose the real Jessica altogether!''

Eight

EYES AND EARS

The halls are buzzing with the news of a hot and heavy thing going on between Lila F. and a certain blond football player. Chalk up one more for Lila. . . . Three cheers for Lois W.! John P. showed up at her party. Guess sometimes dreams *do* come true. . . . Bill C.'s found another surf bunny. . . . Enid R.'s packing up her suitcases for another weekend visit with G.W.—fourth in a row, but who's counting? . . . Cara W. has her eye on a basketball-playing senior. Maybe *she* can get him interested in something besides dribbling! . . . Danger: Toni J.'s now on the roads. Pedestrians beware. . . .

Elizabeth sighed with despair after giving her latest column for *The Oracle* a final read. It seemed to her that it lacked its usual punch. Had her writing gone stale? she wondered. No, the breezy copy was as fast-paced and readable as always. There were plenty of tidbits on all the leading couples in school. All but one. And that, she realized, was where the trouble lay.

Elizabeth had left out the most talked-about duo in school, Jessica and Bruce. Not that there hadn't been anything to write about, she admitted grudgingly to herself. In the two weeks they had been dating, the two had been nearly inseparable around campus, sharing lunches and study periods, frequently cutting classes to sneak some loving moments in the alley behind the school cafeteria. Jessica devotedly went to every single one of Bruce's tennis practices, watching his every shot with adoring eyes. She even ran after his tennis balls as if performing a sacred duty. She spent almost every night with him as well, and when she didn't she kept a vigil by the phone, just in case he had a sudden change in plans.

During dinner the night before, Jessica had given everyone a replay of a practice game between Bruce and another player on the team. "He sounds quite good, Jessica," her father had commented. "But has he been able to beat you, yet?"

"Oh, we don't play against each other."

Ned and Alice Wakefield exchanged puzzled

looks. "You mean you play doubles together?" Mr. Wakefield had asked.

"No."

"Then what?"

"I just watch," she'd declared matter-of-factly—as if it were perfectly normal for the Wakefield family's best tennis player to sit on the sidelines voluntarily.

Her father had stared at her incredulously. "But why, Jess? You love to play."

With that now familiar dreamlike look in her eyes, Jessica had said, "I'd rather watch *him*, Daddy. He looks so beautiful on the courts."

Mr. Wakefield had smiled at his daughter's romantic vision, while his wife had given Elizabeth a worried look.

"Didn't you two play a few sets when you first started going out?" Elizabeth had asked pointedly. "I seem to remember you were looking forward to showing him how good you are."

Jessica had snorted. "That was so juvenile of me. Besides, I could never beat him—he's very, very good."

Now, staring at her column, Elizabeth realized that if she had ever complained about the old Jessica, she'd gladly take it all back now. She couldn't stand the changes Bruce had caused in her sister. The old Jessica was fun-loving, spontaneous—and she *never* walked away from a good game of tennis. And, more importantly, Jessica always shared everything with her. Now, more often than not, Elizabeth had to find out about Jessica's doings from starry-eyed dinner conversations like these—and she didn't like what she was hearing. It was clear that the strong-willed twin she used to know had turned into a helpless puppet—and Bruce Patman was pulling all the strings.

DROIDS DO IT AGAIN
By Elizabeth Wakefield
(second in a continuing series)

The Droids' path to rock-and-roll stardom took them this week to Marshalltown, where they performed at the Rancho East, one of the beach area's leading music spots. We're told that the Sweet Valley band proved once again that they are one of the up-and-coming groups on the rock scene, earning a standing ovation from the enthusiastic audience.

Droids' drummer Emily Mayer summed up her feelings about the show: "It was our best performance yet. Everything seemed to click, and the crowd was super. I wanted to play for them all night."

The band has been on the move since last performing in Sweet Valley. Guy Chesney, keyboardist for the group, has been busy writing original songs, three of which were introduced at Saturday's concert. "We're getting into new areas, away from the simple old love songs," he said. "Topics like alienation and loneliness. They may sound like downers, but the messages are uplifting. And of course there's still the famous Droids beat that Sweet Valleyites know us for."

Tony Conover, The Droids' new manager, plans to continue showcasing the group at clubs around the state. Next week the band returns to Sand Pines, where they made their impressive debut two weeks ago.

"Pretty good write-up, don't you think?" Guy handed the paper to Max for his inspection.

"If you like fiction." Max rolled up the paper and whacked Guy with it. "You're beginning to believe your own notices. That's bad, man."

"Yeah, what about that standing ovation business?" Emily came down from behind her drums and joined the boys as they seated themselves around an old table. "The place was half empty, and Liz wasn't even there, so she had to get the information from somebody. Wonder who?" She looked directly at Guy, who couldn't meet her eyes.

"It's not hurting us, right?" Guy defended his action. "What's wrong with letting everyone in school think we're really making it?"

"Nothing, except it's not true," Dan said.

Max lit up a cigarette. "Yeah, two gigs in dives like those don't qualify as success in my book. When's Tony going to get us some real dates?"

"I thought you didn't care," Emily said. Max just shrugged.

"Did someone mention Tony?" Dana came running down the stairs and took a seat with the others. "Sorry I'm late, but I was on the phone with Tony for a long time. He's in L.A. trying to line us up at more clubs." She smiled. "He says he's getting lots of positive feedback. Isn't that great?"

"Fantastic!" Emily cried. "Where are we playing next?"

"He says he'll get back to me in a day or two." Dana looked at the others. "We ready to get started?"

"Yeah, sure." Suddenly glum, Guy pulled back his chair and walked slowly to his synthesizer.

The sudden change in mood was apparent to Emily. "Are you OK, Guy?" she asked, realizing he might be reading something hurtful into Dana's conversation with Tony.

He turned instead to Dana and asked, "Why did Tony call you? I thought we agreed that I was the one he'd be dealing with."

"Maybe your line was busy," Max said sarcastically.

"I don't know why he called me," Dana answered. "But it doesn't really matter, does it, Guy?"

The frizzy-haired musician switched on his instrument and didn't say another word.

Nine

Jessica arrived at school the following Friday wearing her cheerleading uniform. The football team was playing rival Dallas Heights High that evening, and the whole school was getting ready for the action. Although she'd missed practice for the past three weeks, Jessica was as up for the game as the rest of the squad and couldn't wait for the morning's special assembly to rally team spirit. There'd been some talk of kicking her off the squad for missing so many practices, but Jessica put her old charm to work and wheedled herself back into everybody's good graces. With the entire school planning to attend the home game, this was one event she didn't want to miss.

She ran through the packed hallway to the locker

area to find Bruce, who'd been unable to take her to school that morning because his Porsche was in the shop for repairs. Finding him rummaging through his open locker, she put her hands over his eyes and whispered, "Guess who?"

"I'd know those beautiful hands anywhere. Must be my pretty little princess."

"I should have known I couldn't fool you," Jessica said, giggling.

Bruce turned around, ready to give her a good-morning hug. But he stopped when he saw what she was wearing.

Jessica grew puzzled at the change in his expression. "What's the matter, honey?" she asked.

Bruce's scowl grew deeper. "What's the idea of that outfit?"

"You haven't gone blind all of a sudden, have you?" she teased. "It's my cheerleading outfit. I just had it cleaned. Doesn't it look nice? I wanted to look my best for the assembly and tonight's game." As soon as the words were out, Jessica realized she'd said something wrong. "What's the matter, Bruce? Haven't you ever seen a cheerleader before?"

"Who said you're going to the football game?"

Jessica looked at him disbelievingly. "It's the biggest game of the year. Of course I'm going."

"How come you didn't mention this to me?"

Jessica couldn't understand why Bruce was getting angry with her. "I—I didn't think it was necessary, honey. I mean, you know I'm on the squad, so I just assumed you knew I'd be there."

"Never assume anything with me, babe." Bruce's tone was harsh, unsympathetic. "I thought the two of us would take a drive down to the beach tonight."

"But what about the game?"

"Football bores me. And if you know what's right for us, you'll find a way to miss this game." He put his hands firmly on her shoulders. "Tell me, baby, who'd you rather be with? Me, or a bunch of chicks with fat thighs in short skirts?"

Jessica hated the hard look she saw in Bruce's eyes. Hesitating a moment, she ran her fingers nervously through her hair. "Well, if you put it that way . . ."

Jessica went to the assembly but asked to be excused from English class that morning because of a splitting headache. At lunchtime she passed Lila Fowler in the hall and complained of stomach cramps. By last period she was crying uncontrollably to Cara Walker. She was feeling so awful, she said, she just didn't see how she was going to be able to make it to the game.

By seven o'clock, however, she'd made a miraculous recovery. She was dressed and ready to go when Bruce picked her up for the beach.

* * *

A few days later Cara barged into the newspaper office. Ignoring the meeting in progress between Elizabeth and Mr. Collins, the faculty adviser for the paper, she walked right up between the two. "Your sister is mad," she announced.

Elizabeth looked helplessly at the faculty adviser, who nodded as he rose and left the two girls alone. Elizabeth offered Cara a seat, which she declined. "Who's she mad at?" Elizabeth asked.

"Not mad-angry—mad in the head. Do you know what she just told me? She's quitting the cheerleading squad!"

Elizabeth was truly startled by the news. "She didn't say anything about it to me. Did she tell you why?"

"She says she's tired of it." Cara shrugged. "Maybe she is. She sure has missed a lot of practices lately. But if you ask me, I think Bruce made her quit."

"Or she quit to stay on his good side," Elizabeth thought aloud. "He broke a date with her this week, and I thought she'd go out of her mind."

"Oh, Liz, what are we going to do about her? We've got to get her away from that boy."

"You're not still interested in him, are you?"

Cara rolled her eyes. "Liz, I've been down that road. Once is enough. I like my independence too much."

"So he tried to control you just like he's doing with Jessica?"

"From what I can see, yes. I hardly ever spend time with her these days, though. That girl hasn't been herself since he came on the scene. She's surrendered to him body and soul. And for what? I've heard Bruce hardly spends a dime on her and never takes her anywhere except to the beach."

"That's not true!" Elizabeth emphatically denied the accusation, although she had no way of disproving it. "Jessica wouldn't waste five minutes with someone who didn't want to show her a good time."

Cara arched an eyebrow. "I didn't say anything about not having a good time. All I'm saying is, that girl is headed for trouble!"

"It was so nice of you to invite me over tonight, Jessica," Robin gushed. The two girls were in Jessica's room the following night, sitting at her vanity, an array of blushes, lipsticks, and eyeshadows lined up in front of them.

"When you reminded me of the makeup lesson I promised you, I couldn't say no," Jessica told her, failing to add that Bruce had broken their date that night because of family obligations.

Jessica pulled Robin's hair back from her face. Despite herself she admired the girl's clear complexion and fine bone structure. If Robin lost some weight, she might not be bad-looking, Jessica realized. For a moment she groped for a tactful way of expressing her observation to Robin, then decided to let it pass.

"I was surprised you still wanted to do it," Robin was saying. "I mean, with all the time you've been spending with Bruce lately."

"We can't be together *all* the time. I told Bruce I simply couldn't abandon my friends. Besides, I owe this to you for helping me with my history."

"Oh, that was no problem, and if you need more help with anything, just let me know."

"I'll keep that in mind," Jessica said. She finished dabbing Autumn Smoke eye shadow on Robin's lids. "What do you think?"

"Nice," Robin murmured. Her eyes, however, were locked on the tiny teddy bear with the Pi Beta Alpha T-shirt sitting on the edge of the vanity. Impulsively she picked it up. "He's cute. Does he have a name?"

"Bartholomew."

Robin sighed. "I wish I had one."

Jessica shrugged. "It's just a teddy."

"No, it's a PBA teddy. I'd love to be in the sorority. What do you have to do to join?"

Jessica stared hard at Robin's reflection in the mirror. *The girl can't seriously believe anyone would want a butterball like her as a sorority sister*, Jessica thought. "Sorry, Robin, membership's closed for the year," she told her.

"Really? That's not what Lila Fowler said. I over-heard her at lunch the other day rating potential pledges."

Jessica was ready to stuff her cotton balls into Lila's mouth. "Oh, that's right," she quickly corrected herself. "I've been so caught up in other things I forgot all about the next rush." She carelessly tossed aside the cotton she'd used to wipe the powder off Robin's nose. "It's not so important to me anymore."

"How can you say that? PBA is the most important club around school. I'd do anything to get in."

"Anything, Robin?" A thought flashed through Jessica's mind. Robin's overwhelming desire to get into PBA might be used to her own advantage. Remembering her several household chores, Jessica smiled serenely at Robin. "By the way, how's your cooking?"

"Not bad. I'm pretty good with casseroles and stews."

"Great. See, I want to surprise Bruce with a home-cooked meal sometime, but I'm a terrible cook. Maybe you can come over tomorrow night and show me how to prepare something? Of course, you can stay and eat with us, too."

"I'd love to help," Robin said eagerly.

Jessica smacked her forehead. "Oh, I just re-membered. Bruce wants me to go over to his place for a little while after school. But I shouldn't be there too long. Liz will be here, though, and she'll let you in if I'm not back yet." Jessica smiled to herself, admiring her own cleverness. She had no intention of returning home until right before dinnertime. It would be just perfect to find a hot meal waiting on the table when she arrived.

"That's OK. What will you and Bruce be doing?"

Jessica looked into the mirror and smiled. "That's our secret," she said. "Something special that no one but the two of us can share."

As the weeks went by, Bruce began to come up with more and more reasons why he couldn't see Jessica. His nights were increasingly taken up with important dinners with his father or with school projects that simply had to get done if he had any hope of graduating.

Or so he told Jessica.

Jessica began to realize he was slipping away, so she did all she could to make herself available for him whenever he wanted. At home she sat and waited for the occasional call saying that he was free and ready to share a few hours with her. Most of the time the calls never came, but when they did, Jessica dropped whatever she was doing to be with Bruce.

Their dates almost always consisted of drives to the beach. Jessica loved those times alone with him, but she also longed to do things with the rest of her friends. She hardly ever socialized with them anymore. But whenever she mentioned this to Bruce, he'd scoff at her. "What do you need other people for?" he'd always tell her. "You've got me."

It was Jessica's desire to get more involved with the school scene that caused her first actual fight with Bruce. She was all prepared to go to a sorority dance when Bruce offhandedly informed her that he planned to spend the evening working on his car with a few of his university buddies.

"But you can't do that!" Jessica cried.

"You telling me how to run my life, babe?" he growled at her.

Jessica quickly retreated. "Oh, no, Bruce. I mean, I didn't know you'd made other plans. I just assumed we were going."

"I told you before—never assume anything with me."

"But you knew I wanted to go, Bruce."

"I told you I've got other plans."

"Can't you break them?" she pleaded.

"Nobody tells me what to do, Jessica," he said angrily. "And I don't feel like going to a stupid dance."

"So I'll go without you," she said, the old Jessica surfacing for a fleeting instant.

His eyes bored into her. "You do that, baby, and you just see whose arms you won't be in next Saturday night."

Jessica didn't say another word. The meaning of his threat was clear. Unwilling to risk losing him, she obediently stayed home.

Jessica had grown accustomed to rearranging her life to suit Bruce, but as the days passed she decided to do something to fill those idle hours without him. The following Saturday, when Bruce told her he had to pick up his grandmother from the airport and spend the day with her, she decided to accept a baby-sitting job for Mr. Collins's son, Teddy. Mr. Collins, who was divorced, was so delighted to have his son's favorite baby-sitter back that he didn't mind her special request to have Teddy stay at her house while he ran his errands. Jessica invited Robin to join her. There was always the possibility that Bruce might call, and even Jessica was responsible enough not to leave a six-year-old alone in a strange house. Robin would be her backup in case she had to go.

Jessica found the afternoon insufferable. Teddy was cranky—he had a cold—and was constantly demanding that she entertain him. And Robin was starting to get demanding herself, continually throwing not-so-subtle hints about wanting to join the sorority. Jessica was grateful when Bruce called at three-thirty. He wanted to see her in fifteen minutes.

"I've got an emergency, Robin," she said, white-faced, after she hung up. "It's Bruce. His grand-mother arrived, but she suddenly got sick, and he's a wreck about it. He'd really like me to be with him. Do you mind staying here with Teddy until Mr. Collins gets back?"

Robin minded, but she was afraid to lose what she considered to be Jessica's friendship. "Sure, I'll stay," she said good-naturedly.

Bruce drove Jessica to the Dairi Burger. "A little food always helps when you have some bad news," he said, ordering a cheeseburger and fries for her.

"What is it?" Jessica asked, alarmed. *It must be about his grandmother*, she thought. But Bruce never mentioned his grandmother. Instead, he looked at her sheepishly. "It's about tomorrow. I'm going to have to cancel our date. I'm afraid Dad made plans without telling me. He's throwing a cocktail party for some of his major clients, and he's ordered me to be there and play the obedient son." Bruce made it sound like a fate worse than death. He kissed her forehead lightly. "I'd rather spend the day with you, but when Dad calls, there's no denying him."

Having looked forward to the picnic she'd planned, Jessica was disappointed. She sincerely felt the day alone with him, up in the secluded forestland, was just what was needed to give their relationship new life. But she also saw a way to salvage the day for the two of them. "Tomorrow doesn't have to be a drag for you," she hinted.

"What do you mean?"

"You wouldn't be bored if I was there with you," Jessica said, slipping her arms around his waist.

Bruce pushed her aside. "No, baby," he hedged uncomfortably. "You wouldn't enjoy it."

"Why not?" she asked. The more she thought about the idea, the more she liked it. "I'd love to go to one of your father's parties."

"Tomorrow's not the right time," Bruce said, turning away.

"Why not? Your dad said I was always welcome at your house." Jessica could hear herself pleading, and she hated herself for it. But she was desperate to be with him.

"I said no, Jessica," Bruce insisted angrily. "Forget it."

"Please don't be mad at me, Bruce," Jessica begged in a soft little-girl voice. "I just want to be with you. Don't you understand that?" Tears were brimming just behind her eyelids.

"Sure, baby, sure," he said. "I want to be with you, too." Slowly he lowered his lips until they rested firmly on hers. "Tomorrow may be out, but in the meantime," he breathed, stroking her hair, "there's still the rest of today . . ."

Ten

Elizabeth ran into the newspaper office a few days later and grabbed a copy of the latest *Oracle* from the stacks that covered the two front tables. It always excited her to see the newspaper as soon as it came in. Finding an empty seat in the busy office, she sat down and began to skim the front page.

But she couldn't resist the temptation to look over her own "Eyes and Ears" column first. Her mouth dropped open in shock, however, after she turned the page and spotted an item she had never written. The words jumped out at her as if they were printed in red ink: "And of course our heartiest congrats to Sweet Valley's own Bruce Patman, who took first prize in last Sunday's Sun Desert Road Rally. . . ."

Elizabeth was distraught. It was infuriating that someone had tampered with her column, but she was more upset by the item itself. She was positive Jessica had told her that Bruce had spent that day with his parents. Either somebody was playing a joke on Bruce—or he had lied to Jessica.

She had to find out the truth. She asked around, but no one in the office at the time knew anything about the item, and the one person who was sure to know—the editor, Penny Ayala—was home sick with the flu.

That night Elizabeth decided to ask Jessica if she knew what had happened.

"Oh, I know all about that." Jessica tossed her head lightly. "Bruce lent his car to Paul Sherwood, and he was the one who won the rally. Somebody on the newspaper just got their facts mixed up."

"And put them into *my* column?" Elizabeth looked skeptically at her sister.

"I don't know anything about that," Jessica insisted. "All I know is that Bruce definitely wasn't at the rally. He was home with his parents."

Elizabeth looked sadly at her sister. Jessica was a marvelous actress, but even *she* couldn't mask the uncertainty she had to be feeling about Bruce's story. Her attitude made Elizabeth all the more certain that Bruce wasn't playing straight with her twin. "Are you sure he was there, Jess?"

"Why would he lie?" Jessica questioned, ignoring the hundreds of times *she'd* stretched the truth

101

to protect herself. "And if it turned out he *was* at that rally, so what? It would just mean his plans changed. I can't know *everything* he does. I don't have a leash on him, you know."

"I know," Elizabeth said gently, "but sometimes I think he's got one around you."

"That's garbage!"

"Is it?" Elizabeth challenged, not caring that she was losing control. "What about the way he reacted to your wanting to go to that sorority dance?"

"He was just feeling jealous. I think he was afraid for me to go on my own. He doesn't want to lose me, and I had no right to make the entire situation so difficult for him."

"Come on, Jessica, you had *every* right to go. Stop making excuses for him. Besides, he'd made other plans that night. What were you supposed to do, sit home and count the dots on your wallpaper?"

"If that's what he wanted me to do, yes," Jessica said stubbornly.

Elizabeth shook her head and sighed. "I don't know what's happened to you, Jess. Don't you see how ridiculous that is?"

"Nothing Bruce wants is ridiculous," Jessica countered. "You don't understand how it is to be really in love with someone. I'm willing to make whatever sacrifices I have to in order to please Bruce. Are you going to tell me you don't ever go out of your way for Todd?"

"I do," Elizabeth responded. "I do, but not at the expense of my own life. Believe me, I know you really care about Bruce, but you can't just give up everything else because of it."

"I'll give up what I think I should," Jessica replied stiffly.

"He may not be worth it," Elizabeth said sadly.

"Well, it's not for you to decide." Jessica's expression hardened. "You just let me be the judge of that, big sister."

Jessica met Robin by her locker after school the following day. "I know it's short notice," she said in a hushed voice, "but I have a feeling you're going to like what I have to tell you. After doing a lot of thinking, I've decided you'd be a perfect candidate for PBA."

Robin's eyes sparkled with happiness. "Jessica, that's terrific!" She made a move to wrap her arms around her friend, but Jessica grabbed her by the wrists and stopped her.

"Not so fast, dear. You see, there's a catch. Some of the girls in the sorority don't think you're ready for us yet. Of course, I told them they were mistaken, but they insisted on a little test to prove your worthiness. If I were you, I'd be insulted and forget the whole thing, but I guess you'll have to make up your own mind."

Robin shook her head emphatically. She'd be a

fool to turn her back on the opportunity she'd dreamed of. Whatever it was they wanted couldn't be that bad. "I'll do it."

"But you don't even know what it is!"

"It doesn't matter. Tell me what it is," Robin demanded.

"If you insist." Jessica gave her a look of pity, but inside she was delighted that Robin had fallen for her story. "Mr. Russo keeps a stack of papers in the third drawer of the big glass cabinet in the chemistry lab. The drawer is locked, but the key is in the side compartment of his desk, taped to the top of the drawer. You're to take one of the papers marked test number three and bring it back to me."

Robin hedged. This wasn't a silly little rush prank. "I don't know, Jessica. That sounds like cheating—not to mention stealing."

"Oh, no!" Jessica said emphatically. "Would I ask you to do this if the paper really meant anything?"

"But what if I get caught?"

"You won't. Bruce assures me it's foolproof."

"Bruce? What's he got to do with it?"

Jessica hesitated a second. She shouldn't have mentioned Bruce's name in connection with this scheme, but it was too late to take it back. "Oh, he once made some fraternity buddies do something just like this," she said, covering herself. "They got away with it—and so will you if you follow my plan. All you have to do is hide out in the second-floor bathroom till dusk. Everyone will be gone by then, but there will still be enough light to see by. Get the test, then leave through the back entrance." She stopped; it was a calculated pause. "But of course I wouldn't want you to risk it if you don't want to."

"You say I have to do this to get into the sorority?"

"If you pull it off, I promise I'll nominate you."

Robin toyed with her combination lock as she weighed the consequences. True, there was a chance she could get caught, but it seemed a small risk compared to the reward. Turning from her locker, she nodded determinedly at Jessica. "When do I have to do it?"

"Tonight. And after you've got it, bring it over to my house. Understand?"

At seven that evening Robin stopped by Jessica's house, clutching a brown envelope tightly against her body. "I've got it," she whispered conspiratorially as soon as Jessica opened the door.

Jessica breathed a sigh of relief. "Good," she said. "Now there's one more thing you have to do."

Robin frowned. Alone in the darkened school, she'd been scared half to death. Her heartbeat hadn't returned to normal until she'd pulled up safely in front of Jessica's house. She never wanted to go through anything like that again. In fact, right this minute she couldn't understand where her brains had been in the first place when she agreed to the prank. "What now?" she asked reluctantly, handing the envelope to Jessica.

But Jessica refused to take it. "Don't give it to me. Tomorrow morning slip it inside Emily Mayer's locker."

"Emily? I didn't know she was in PBA."

"She wants to join," Jessica said, knowing full well that The Droids' drummer wasn't the slightest bit interested in the sorority. "We have something in mind for her."

"Whatever you say, Jess." Robin sighed in relief. After what she'd just gone through, Jessica's new request would be easy.

Before class the following morning, Jessica approached Emily in the hallway. "You look pretty tired," she noted with false sympathy. "I'll bet you've been very busy with The Droids."

"Yeah, I have," Emily answered offhandedly. "Two shows every weekend and practice every night."

"Too busy to study much, I imagine."

Emily looked at her strangely. Jessica hardly ever spoke to her unless she wanted something. "Right. Why do you ask?"

"Are you ready for the big test tomorrow morning?"

Emily hesitated before answering. The Droids' practice schedule had taken up so much of her time that she'd had no chance to study. But that morning she'd discovered an envelope containing the test in her locker. Had Jessica put it there? "I don't know," she hedged. "There's so much to study."

"You're a good person, Emily, and I'd hate to see you go nuts over the books when you don't have to."

"I'm touched by your concern," Emily said stiffly.

Jessica, pleased with Emily's responses so far, decided to get right to the point. "I know you have tomorrow's test."

"Because you put it in my locker, right?"

"I don't have the faintest idea where you got it," Jessica lied, "but I saw you looking at it this morning—with my very own eyes."

"What makes you think I'm going to use it?" Emily challenged her.

"Why wouldn't you, Emily? You flunked the last test. And I'm sure you'd much rather practice with the band tonight than cram in eight chapters of that junk. Face it, Emily, the test is a godsend."

"You're talking about cheating, Jessica."

"Maybe *you'd* call it that. *I'd* call it your golden opportunity. C'mon, Emily, do you really want to see the look on your parents' faces when you come home with another F? Especially when you don't have to?"

Emily's eyes narrowed. "What's in it for you, Jessica?"

"Not much. Just a passing grade. See, Russo would know something was wrong if I aced this test all of a sudden. But he wouldn't question an A from you. And all you have to do to get an A is to figure out the answers to the test. That shouldn't be hard for a brain like you."

"And you plan to copy the answers off my paper," Emily finished.

"Not all of them," Jessica corrected her. "Just enough to pass."

"And what if I decide not to use the test?"

"You can't afford not to use it," she threatened. "I know a certain teacher who'd be pretty upset if he knew you had the exam in your hands. You wouldn't want him to find out, would you?"

Several days later Elizabeth pulled her mother's red Fiat Spider up to Max Dellon's house after school. As part of her continuing series on The Droids, she planned to get a behind-the-scenes look at how they prepared for their concerts.

Max let her in and led her to one of two beat-up couches leaning against the back wall of the basement. The rest of the group were busily tuning their instruments. "We were just getting ready to start," he explained.

Elizabeth shook her head. "Go on with what you're doing and try to pretend I'm not here. I'll save my questions for after you're done." She sat down and reached into her shoulder bag for her little spiral notebook.

Max shrugged nonchalantly. "Fine with me."

The basement, set up like a mini-studio, was hardly the wild place Elizabeth had heard so much about. No mattresses on the floor, no smoke choking up the room—just the band instruments, a couch, a table and a couple of chairs, plenty of posters, and a tiny refrigerator in the corner. Elizabeth noted all this in her book as she listened to the overpowering sound of the band.

The Droids really did act as if Elizabeth weren't there. Midway through the second song, Guy walked away from his synthesizer in a huff, angry over the way Dana was singing. Dana couldn't see what he was upset about, and the two of them got into a shouting match that lasted five minutes. Max seemed to find the spat amusing, and every now and then he'd interject a remark that got the fireworks going all over again. For the rest of the set, Max played his guitar as if he couldn't care less, and while it sounded fine to Elizabeth, she could tell there was something missing in his spirit.

During the rest of the hour-long session, the

tight expression on Guy's face revealed his unhappiness with the band's sound. He made no further interruptions, though. After their signature song, "Looking Through the Lies," he called for a break, and the tired fivesome came down off the platform, taking seats around Elizabeth.

Max stopped first at the refrigerator and took out some cans of soft drinks for everyone. "That's a Tab for you," he said, handed the can to Dana. "Cokes for you, my dear Emily, and for you, Danny boy." He handed them to his playing partners. "And an orange soda for you, my man." Max thrust the can into Guy's hand. "What can I get you, Liz?"

"A root beer if you have it. I see you've got everyone's taste covered here."

"Have to in order to survive," Max said, handing over her drink. "When you spend nearly every waking hour with these bozos, you end up learning a lot about them."

"Sometimes more than you want to know," Emily grumbled, aiming her gaze at Guy.

"Your time together has paid off, I think," Elizabeth said to the group. "You sounded terrific."

"Thanks, Liz," Guy said. "But we have a long way to go. We're still not as tight as we have to be."

"Come on, Guy, don't hang our dirty laundry in front of the press," Dana shot back, only half joking. She was still upset over his earlier criticism. Turning to Elizabeth, she explained, "Guy is a perfectionist. One wrong note and he goes nuts. But Tony—our manager, you know—agrees with you. He says we're sounding better and better all the time."

"So why does he keep booking us in those hole-in-the-wall places?" Guy complained.

"Guy, come off it," Emily interrupted. "You know as well as we all do that we're not going to make it overnight. We need to play these places for the experience. And Tony's promised to get us into bigger spots as soon as he can. You've just got to have faith in him. Right, Dana?"

The lead singer looked at Emily a little shakily, obviously not sure how to answer. "Oh, uh, right, Emily. Tony's going to make us hit big." Elizabeth thought she sounded strangely unconvinced.

"*Do* you trust your manager?" Elizabeth asked her.

"Of course," Dana said hurriedly. "He's been very good to us. In fact, there's a chance we'll be playing a small club in L.A. in a couple of weeks."

The rest of the group looked at her in astonishment. "You dreaming, girl?" Dan asked.

"That's the word I got from Tony," Dana insisted.

"When did you talk to him?" Guy demanded angrily.

"Last night after practice."

"Why didn't you tell the rest of us about this sooner? Didn't you think we'd be interested?" Guy continued his inquisition.

"I thought you knew. Tony told me he was going to call you."

"I guess he forgot," Guy said disgustedly. "Just like he forgot to tell me about the change in this week's date."

"What are you driving at, Guy?" Dana probed.

"Why don't you tell me?" Guy shot back. "Since when did you appoint yourself group spokesman? Why is Tony letting only you in on all his wonderful plans for us?"

Elizabeth was getting very uncomfortable with the mounting tension in the room. "I—I think I'd better go now," she said, rising.

Dan turned to Guy. "Hey, you've driven away the press. We're never going to get anywhere with that kind of attitude."

"Forget it, Dan," Elizabeth said. "I'll be back. I see I've caught you on a bad day."

Out of Elizabeth's earshot Dana whispered, "Every day's a bad day lately."

"Maybe you're right, Liz," Max said diplomatically. "I think we can all use a break. What do you say, bozos? Let's cool it for now and start up again tonight."

Guy agreed reluctantly, and Dan and the two girls followed suit.

As Elizabeth neared the door, Emily asked her for a lift home. "I usually go with Dana, but there's something I want to talk to you about."

Together they walked slowly to Elizabeth's car. "If it's about the article," she said, "don't worry. I can see you guys are pretty tense, and having me around probably didn't help. I'll hold off on the piece until you're more relaxed."

Emily smiled. "Thanks, but that's not what I had in mind."

"What is it then?"

Emily didn't answer until they were both in the car and on the road. Alone with Elizabeth, she was suddenly unsure whether she wanted to bring up the subject at all. But the longer she sat silent, the more the need to talk rose up inside her. Finally, about two blocks from her house, she burst out, "Liz, have you ever felt really dishonest?"

"Hasn't everyone at one point or another?"

"I mean, have you ever gone through with anything that you knew from the very beginning wasn't good, or right?"

"Why do you ask?"

Emily bit her lip. "I kind of cheated on Russo's test."

"Oh, boy."

"I know," Emily agreed. "It's a big one. And I never would have done it if—" Emily stopped herself. She had a powerful need to confess everything, but she didn't want to tell on Jessica, especially not to her sister.

Elizabeth misread her hesitation. "You don't have to tell me. I can see the pressure you've been under with The Droids and everything."

"That doesn't excuse what I did. I'm really ashamed of myself, Liz. I've never done anything like this before."

"Why are you telling *me*, Emily?"

"I don't know. I guess because I trust you, Liz. And I don't know what to do. I thought you could help."

Elizabeth tapped the steering wheel as she chose her words. "Well, I guess one thing you could do is tell Russo the truth. But, boy, that'll take a lot of guts."

"I can't do that."

"Yeah, I don't blame you for feeling that way, but I bet you'll end up a lot happier about things if you can get the truth out. I know you well enough to know you couldn't live with something like that hanging over your head."

"But he'll flunk me!"

"He'll be angry, but I don't think he'd flunk you just like that. Russo's tough, but he's a human being, too. He might understand everything you've been going through lately and accept what made you cheat. You've got a good reputation at school, and he'll have a lot more sympathy for

114

you if you tell him now than he will if you don't tell him and he finds out anyway."

Emily quietly considered Elizabeth's words. Finally, as they pulled into the Mayers' driveway, Emily turned to Elizabeth and gave her a trembling smile. "Thanks, Liz, I'll think about what you said."

Elizabeth watched her troubled friend disappear into the house and shook her head sympathetically. *This is one problem I'm glad I don't have*, she thought. *It's going to be tough to settle. Very tough.*

Eleven

The Sweet Valley High newspaper office was buzzing with the frenetic activity that was standard on the day before presstime. Each of the page editors was stationed at his or her desk, marking last-minute changes in the copy. Penny sat at a table in the front of the room, talking with Mr. Collins about the upcoming issue.

Elizabeth walked in with her latest "Eyes and Ears" column and waited until the faculty adviser was finished before approaching the *Oracle*'s editor. "Excuse me, Penny, I have something for you."

Penny grabbed a tissue and blew her nose. "Sorry. This cold is dragging on forever." Quickly she looked over the pages Elizabeth had dropped on her desk. "Great. By the way, I didn't have a chance to tell you before, but last week's column was very good—as usual."

This was the opening Elizabeth was waiting for. "The part I wrote, or the part you slipped in without telling me?"

"What part, Liz?"

Elizabeth felt her patience wearing thin. "Don't play games with me, too, Penny. You're not like that."

"And you're not the type to go around accusing someone," Penny shot back, reaching for another tissue. "Would you mind telling me what you're talking about?"

"You really don't know?" Elizabeth pulled up a chair and sat down. "Someone added an item to my column after I handed it in. Everyone around here denied doing it, so I assumed it must have been you. I'm sorry if I'm wrong."

"Apologies accepted." Penny sneezed. "Excuse me. I never tamper with other people's copy without good reason . . . and certainly not without telling them first. What's got you so upset?"

Elizabeth showed her the item about Bruce's road rally win. Penny put it down and laughed. "You ought to know better than to think I'd give that creep any excess publicity. . . . But I know someone who would." Turning toward the back of the room, she shouted as loudly as her hoarse voice would allow. "John Pfeifer. Up here now!"

The sports editor squeezed his broad frame

around a few empty chairs to the front desk. "What can I do for you, chief?" he asked good-naturedly.

"John," Penny began, "let's get right to the point. Why did you tell me Liz wanted this item about Bruce Patman put into her column?"

John looked at Penny, then at Elizabeth, then at the floor. He was caught in a lie, and there was no way out but the truth. "Bruce is always getting on my case about not featuring him enough in the paper, so I thought I'd do him a favor and drop this in. I didn't have any more room on the sports page, and I didn't think Liz would mind."

"Well, I did," Elizabeth said.

John smiled ruefully. "So did Bruce, as it turned out. He had a fit when he read that." He turned to Penny. "Are you through with me now?"

"For the moment."

"John, wait a minute." Elizabeth pulled him over to the wall next to the blackboard. "You say Bruce was the one driving his car?"

"Of course. You don't think he'd let anyone else behind the wheel, do you?"

Elizabeth had doubted that he would, but John had confirmed her secret fear. "Was anyone in the car with him?" She almost hated to hear the answer.

"Yes, his navigator."

"Who was it?" Elizabeth pressed on.

John suspected he'd said too much. He looked at the floor again. "I—I don't know."

"You don't know—or you can't tell me? Which is it, John?"

There was a long moment before he slowly raised his eyes to meet Elizabeth's. "I—I can't tell you," he admitted.

"Thanks, John." Elizabeth heaved a sigh. "That's all I needed to know."

Elizabeth went over the conversation with John a hundred times in her head as she sat in her room that evening. Actually it was what John hadn't said that had her so concerned. She had assumed all along that Bruce was at that road rally, no matter what he had told Jessica. But she hadn't considered the possibility that he was there with someone else. She had no idea who it might be, but from John's reluctance to talk, she was sure it was another girl.

The road rally incident was her proof that she'd been right all along, that Bruce was indeed not to be trusted. Though she'd hoped for something like this to happen, her unhappiness was overwhelming. It would only be a matter of time before Jessica learned the truth about her beloved Bruce. And when she fell, she was going to fall very hard.

Elizabeth tried to think of a way to save her sister from that hurt, but realized she was the wrong one to break the news. Not only wouldn't

Jessica believe her, but if Elizabeth dared suggest that Bruce was less than the god Jessica thought he was, her sister was certain to shut her out of her life again.

A knock on Elizabeth's door interrupted her thoughts. "Liz, may I come in?"

Jessica. Elizabeth couldn't help but smile at the irony. Before Bruce came along, Jessica never thought of knocking first, though Elizabeth had often asked her to. "Sure, the door's open."

She had a dress over one arm. "Look what I bought today." She held it up. It was a black crepe de chine dress with a low-cut front and back. "Isn't it beautiful?"

"Very sophisticated. What's the occasion?"

"Just the biggest night of the year. Bruce's birthday, next weekend. Liz, it's going to be soooo special," Jessica cooed.

"With that dress, I wouldn't be surprised."

"Bruce promised me a night to remember. Just the two of us. We'll be starting off with a very quiet, very intimate dinner at the country club. And then after that—who knows?"

"What?" Elizabeth gasped. She'd known for days that Bruce had invited half the school to a big bash in his honor at the country club. She also knew that he'd asked that it be a surprise for Jessica; a special, secret treat. Elizabeth had been astonished that Bruce was going out of his way to have Jessica share in his birthday glory. Now she realized the little bit of credit she'd given him was too much. This was just the easiest way for Bruce to back out of his promise for an intimate evening for two—by simply not telling Jessica until it was too late. Jessica was sure to find out—and then what? It was beyond belief that he could promise her sister a romantic night alone and then spring a cast of thousands on her.

"Oh, I know you're surprised," Jessica said, misinterpreting her sister's stunned expression. "You've probably been thinking that since Bruce and I haven't been seeing each other every night, we'd sort of cooled off. But just the opposite has happened. In fact"—her eyes widened—"I have a feeling Bruce wants to get more serious with me."

"I don't believe it."

"Believe what you will," Jessica said. "But wait and see. He said he has a big surprise planned for me—and I can't wait."

Elizabeth had the dreadful feeling that Bruce's surprise was going to lead to Jessica's heartbreak. "Jess, there's something I—"

Elizabeth was cut short by another knock on the door. "Come on in," Jessica called. "It's open."

It was Cara. "Hope you don't mind my barging in, Liz."

"Of course she doesn't," Jessica cut in. "You're just in time to see the dress I got for Bruce's birthday." She held it up against her body.

"It's beautiful," Cara said. "Bruce'll love it." She gave her friend a big hug.

Jessica was pleased with Cara's reaction. "We'll leave you alone with your books, Liz. Cara and I are going downstairs. She's going to help me figure out how to make a very special birthday cake for a very special boy."

It's just as well I kept my mouth shut, Elizabeth thought after they left. *Jessica would never have believed me.*

How could he do this to me! Jessica fumed inwardly. Never had anyone humiliated her so deeply. And she had gone to so much trouble to make sure that everything would go smoothly.

All through chemistry class she glared at the big red F and the words "See me" scrawled across the top of her last test. Totally ignoring Mr. Russo's lecture on solubility, she tried to figure out what had gone wrong. The plan had been so perfect. Emily had done her part, right down to giving Jessica the thumbs-up sign right before the test. That left only one other possibility: Robin had messed up the papers when she had swiped the test and left a trail of evidence a mile wide. Jessica sighed in disgust. She knew she shouldn't have trusted Robin with such a serious mission. That girl couldn't do anything right.

There was only one thing Jessica could do—tell

Russo that Robin had stolen the test. But right before class ended, she realized she couldn't do that. Not if she wanted Bruce. Once Robin's back was to the wall, Jessica was sure she'd blab everything to Russo, including Bruce's part in the plan.

And if that happened, Jessica concluded, Bruce would never forgive her.

For once in her life she saw no way out of her predicament but the truth—at least partially. She would say she got the answers by looking at Emily's test paper. Steeling herself to accept her punishment, she went up to the chemistry teacher after class, meekly putting the test paper on his desk. "I'd like to explain, Mr. Russo."

"You failed the test, Jessica," he said sternly. "There is no explanation for lack of preparation. Not in this class."

Jessica pursed her lips. "You're right, Mr. Russo," she began apologetically. "I never should have thought I could have gotten away with it. I—"

"There's no excuse for not studying, Jessica," Mr. Russo lectured. "This is the second test in a row you've failed. If your grades don't pick up in a big way, you're looking at an F for the entire term."

Jessica couldn't believe her ears. Russo didn't know she'd copied the answers from Emily. Still appropriately apologetic, she changed gears, opting for another version of the truth. "I want to do well in chemistry, really I do, but I have so much trouble understanding it. And I feel a lot of pressure from home, too. My parents really want me to succeed."

"If you were having trouble, you should have come to me for help earlier. There's still time for you to pass the course, but it's going to take a lot of work. You'll have to pass the rest of the tests this term and do several special assignments. Come see me after class tomorrow and I'll have them ready for you."

Outside in the hallway a few minutes later, Jessica caught up with Emily. Pinning the petite girl up against the cinder-block wall, she looked down at her and hissed, "You double-crossed me, Mayer."

"No, I didn't, Jessica," Emily said defiantly. "And if you don't believe me, go ahead and tell Russo I had the test if you want. But it won't make a difference. He already knows."

Jessica's eyes nearly popped out. "He does?"

"You don't have to worry. I didn't tell him about you—and I won't. But I couldn't live with having cheated, so I told him. He yelled a lot and gave me detention and a pile of special assignments—but crazy as it sounds, I feel relieved."

"That still doesn't explain why I flunked. What happened?"

"I didn't do well, either. At the last minute, Russo made some changes in the test and printed up a whole new batch of them. He said this test

124

was too much like last year's. If you ask me, Jessica, you're lucky he didn't notice you made the same mistakes I made."

Even though she realized she'd gotten off easy, Jessica was still furious at lunchtime as she headed for the cafeteria. She was no better off now than she'd been when she'd first schemed to get the test answers, and now she had a pile of work to do on top of everything else. This wasn't the way it was supposed to turn out.

Only Bruce could tear her mind away from this predicament, and Jessica found him sitting at a table on the patio with his tennis teammates, Tom McKay and John Pfeifer. She could hear him leading the laughter. Bruce had been grouchy when he had spoken with her the night before, and she was glad to see he was in better spirits.

Walking softly so Bruce wouldn't hear her, Jessica made her way to the table, stopping directly behind him. Putting her tray down on a nearby table, she reached over his neck and gave him a big hug. "Hi, there," she purred.

Bruce nonchalantly released her grip on him. "Not now, babe. So, John," he continued as if she weren't there, "I'm behind this guy fifteen-forty, and he's sure he's going to get me on my next serve. But I'm not going to let him get away with it, so I blow him off the court with three straight aces. You should have seen his face!"

"Bruce, can I talk to you for a minute?"

"Can't it wait, Jess? I'm busy."

"But, Bruce! It's about chemistry and—"

"You still hung up on that junk, Jess? I'm bored with it." Abruptly he turned back to his friends. "So then it's his turn to serve, and he's real nervous now. . . ."

Jessica didn't hear the rest of what Bruce was saying. Her mind was too focused on the anger rising inside her. She was sure, had the situation been reversed, she would have listened sympathetically to Bruce's problem. Still, she insisted to herself in an effort to calm down, she *did* interrupt his conversation. That in itself *was* rude. But her anger returned moments later in full force. It was rude, but *not that* rude. Swiftly, Jessica turned to face Bruce with her fury, but one long look at his rugged, handsome face and she chose to contain herself. *I'll get over it*, she thought, sighing. *I hope.*

Twelve

Jessica stood before the bathroom mirror putting the finishing touches on her makeup. The line she drew around her lips with her deep rose liner gave her lower lip the pouty look Bruce found so appealing. With her hair piled high on her head and her body poured into the tight black dress she'd bought especially for that night, Jessica was seduction personified—and she knew it. "If this doesn't get Bruce's heart pumping, the guy has ice water for blood," she told her reflection. Tonight she planned to go all out to make things between Bruce and her perfect again, and her outfit was guaranteed to get things off to a fast start.

After dabbing on a healthy amount of Bruce's

favorite cologne in all the right places, she gathered the half dozen gift boxes she'd so carefully wrapped and carried them downstairs to the front hallway. Excited about the glorious night to come, Jessica waited for her boyfriend to arrive.

Fifteen anxious minutes later the black Porsche pulled up in front of the Wakefield house. Without even waiting for the beep of the horn, Jessica let herself out and ran as fast as she could to the car. "Hi, Bruce," she said, smiling. "Happy birthday."

Bruce leaned across to the passenger side and opened the door. Jessica slid in, resting the packages on her lap. "These for me?" he asked offhandedly.

"They're all for you, birthday boy."

"Great." Casually he tossed them into the back of the car.

That wasn't the reaction Jessica had expected. "Aren't you going to open them?"

"Later." He kissed her lightly on the forehead. "In the meantime let's have some fun." He kissed her again, this time straight and hard on the lips.

Jessica's carefully drawn pout was smudged— and her ego was bruised. She felt he could at least have said something about the way she looked before getting physical. "Aren't you going to say anything about my dress?" she asked.

Bruce gave her a long, lingering once-over.

"Delicious, baby. But you're going to be a little overdressed for the party."

"What party?" Jessica asked, astonished.

"That's the surprise I told you about. It's going to be great, baby. Lots of food, lots of music, everyone from school—"

"But I thought it was going to be just the two of us," Jessica whined, seeing her plans for a private celebration dissolve in the cool evening air.

Bruce tapped the steering wheel and chuckled. "Come on, Jess, I did it for you. You're the one who wanted to do more things with the gang. I told everyone not to tell you. I thought you'd be real happy! Besides, you didn't think I'd let my eighteenth birthday pass unnoticed, did you?"

"You said you wanted to spend it with me," she said softly, her lower lip beginning to tremble. "An intimate night. You promised."

"And that's exactly what we'll have," he said, leering. "After the party. Like down at the beach, for instance?" Taking his right hand off the stick shift, he ran it down Jessica's half-covered thigh.

The private dining room where Bruce's party was being held was already filled close to capacity by the time Bruce and Jessica arrived. "Here's the party boy!" Ken Matthews shouted. A chorus of "Happy Birthday" followed.

Jessica sang along with the others as she watched

129

Bruce beam in delight. He was clearly in his element, the star of the evening, and Jessica had the sickening feeling that he loved it more than any moment the two of them had ever shared.

But she quickly put that out of her mind as Bruce led her over to a table near the empty band platform. "The best seat in the house," he told her. Leaning over her chair, he added, "I've got to make the rounds. Be back as soon as I can."

As Bruce mingled with his guests, Jessica sat alone, trying her best to appear totally unconcerned with his absence. She took her lipstick out of her black satin evening purse and redrew the line on her lower lip. But she couldn't spend all night fixing her makeup, and after a few minutes of examining the contents of her purse, she sat back and peered into the crowd impatiently.

She groaned inwardly when Robin Wilson cut through the crowd and headed for her table. Bruce really *had* invited everybody.

"Oooh, Jessica, you look gorgeous!" Robin gushed.

Jessica couldn't force herself to return the compliment. Wearing a pink-and-white striped dress—horizontal stripes, no less—Robin looked like the poster girl for a cotton candy company. "What are you doing here?" Jessica asked grumpily.

"I couldn't believe it when Bruce invited me. He wanted me to come because I was your special friend. Isn't this place heaven? Everyone's here!"

You can say that again, Jessica thought, staring at the table where Bruce was chatting with a few of the girls from the cheerleading squad. Did he still think of them as "chicks with fat thighs"? she wondered.

"I'm going to check out the food," Robin told her. "See you later."

Elizabeth arrived not too long afterward with Todd. She was shocked to see her sister sitting by herself. "I've got to talk to her," she told Todd.

"Are you sure? The ice princess doesn't look like she wants to be bothered," Todd said.

"Oh, Todd, stop being so hard on her," Elizabeth said. Pointing to the buffet table near the window, she remarked, "Look, there's Winston over by the hors d'oeuvres. Why don't you go keep him company? I'll be back in a minute." She gave him a quick kiss on the cheek before easing her way between the tables to her twin.

Jessica smiled warmly at her sister and admired the teal-blue, cowl-necked dress she had on. "You look great, Liz. It's a wonderful party, isn't it?"

Elizabeth was surprised to find Jessica in such a good mood. "I guess it is," she managed to say.

"Yes, I told Bruce having a party for everyone was the only way to celebrate his birthday. It was great of you to try and keep it a surprise for me."

"You mean you *knew* about this party?" Elizabeth was astonished.

"Well, not really," Jessica faltered. "But I'm very

131

happy about it. I love being with all my friends. Anyway, more than anything, I wanted to look perfect for Bruce—and I think I did a pretty good job, don't you agree?"

Elizabeth was near tears as she listened to Jessica trying to cover up for Bruce. She almost let loose with another angry tirade against her sister's selfish boyfriend, but she realized her words would only fall on deaf ears. "Where is Bruce, anyway?" she asked instead.

"You can't expect him to hang on my arm all night, not when he has all these guests to entertain," Jessica answered defensively, scanning the room for him. Just then The Droids came bounding onto the stage and began tuning up. "There he is now!" Jessica said excitedly.

Elizabeth followed her sister's gaze. "I hope you have a good time tonight, Jess," she said, hoping against hope that her worst fears about Bruce were unfounded. "I've got to talk to Emily. See you later."

After Emily finished adjusting her drum set, Elizabeth asked, "What happened to your club date? I thought you were playing out at the beach tonight."

"Canceled," Emily said, and from the expression on her face, she didn't seem upset about it at all.

"What happened?"

Emily shook her head ruefully. "We were duped.

Tony never had any intention of leading us to the big time."

"I thought he was legitimate."

"We thought so, too, but it seems Guy didn't check hard enough into his background. Tony really did work at that management company he told us about—only they fired him about a month before he came to us. For incompetence. He happened to know the guys who own those two places we played at, but it turns out that music wasn't even the reason he got involved with us in the first place."

"Then what was?" Elizabeth asked.

Emily looked sheepishly at Elizabeth. "He had the hots for Dana," she confided. "For weeks he kept calling her—and driving Guy nuts in the process—and we couldn't figure out why. Dana didn't say anything to us until the other day when he finally tried to score with her. She said no way and threw him out. We haven't heard from him since."

"You don't seem too broken up about it."

"Funny, isn't it?" Emily said. "We spent all that time working our tails off, and now that it's over, do you know what we're all feeling? Relief. Remember that day you came over to watch us rehearse, and you thought you'd caught us on a bad day? It was like that *every* day. We were always on each other's nerves, criticizing every wrong note, every false move. It wasn't fun anymore. We talked it over afterward, and we all agreed if that's what getting to the top is all about, then we're just not ready for it yet. We're better off hanging around Sweet Valley and playing at school and stuff like this party."

"So you're not disappointed?"

"Sure," Emily said wistfully. "I'm disappointed. But at least now I'll have the time to do those chemistry projects for Mr. Russo. Some consolation, huh?"

"I guess that's show business," Elizabeth quipped.

In the meantime someone had noticed the empty chair next to Jessica—Winston. He still cared deeply for her, and more than anything, he wanted her to be happy. Knowing Jessica, he couldn't believe she could enjoy being by herself in the middle of a crowd. After helping himself to some punch, he meandered around the room trying to get up the courage to approach her. By the time he did, The Droids had played several numbers, and the dance floor was packed with couples.

"Uh, the lady looks like she could use a dance partner."

Jessica turned away from the dancing area, where she'd watched Bruce take the floor with Lila Fowler for the second time. "Sorry, Win, I'm sitting this one out."

"I've been practicing a lot since last time we danced."

134

"Good for you, Win. There's always room for improvement."

"That's my line," he said, grinning. "Actually, I'm OK as long as I have space out there to do my stuff on the fast dances. Want to see?"

"I'll watch," she said curtly.

"Come on, Jessica," he urged. "I'll even throw in a few handstands and cartwheels. But I need you up there with me. What do you say? Just one dance."

"Sorry, Win," she repeated. "Bruce promised me the next dance, and this one's almost over. I think you're going to have to do your cartwheels solo."

He remained undaunted. "How about the one after that?"

"Not tonight. And I think you'd better leave now," she whispered. "Bruce is coming over here, and he's not going to like your talking to me."

"Well, excuse me for going near the big shot's property. See you around, Jessica." Thrusting his hands into his jacket pockets, Winston walked away in a huff. He sought out Elizabeth and Todd at the buffet table. "Your sister's impossible," he grumbled to Elizabeth. "Doesn't she realize he's ignoring her?"

"Don't look now, you two," Todd said, "but the party boy's suddenly remembered he came with a date."

Bruce unbuttoned his shirt collar as he approached Jessica. "Hey, baby, having a good time?"

Her heart melted. "The best," she purred, "now that you're here. Have a seat."

Bruce put his arm on her shoulder and gave it a little rub. "Gee, I'm sorry, Jessica, but I promised the next dance to Caroline. You understand, don't you?"

"Certainly, Bruce. I understand completely," she said with false sweetness he did not pick up on. The rage she had felt when he ignored her problem with Mr. Russo began to return. *What*, she thought, *is going on here?*

Bruce didn't ignore Jessica totally, however. During the last dance of the evening, a slow ballad, he held her tightly and nibbled at her ear. *This is more like it*, Jessica thought, her anger starting to subside.

"What do you say we blow this place?" Bruce whispered. "It's getting too formal for me."

"Where to, Bruce? The beach?"

He chuckled. "I like the way you think, babe. But first I want to grab a bite at Guido's. The food here stinks."

"You're going to leave your own party?"

"No, baby, I'm taking the party with me."

"I'm ready whenever you are," she said, looking adoringly into his eyes.

Less than ten minutes later the two of them

were nestled in Bruce's Porsche, heading down the winding, hilly road to Guido's Pizza Palace in the heart of town, a caravan of cars following them to the party's next location.

Thirteen

Bruce's crowd took up an entire section of Guido's, a popular hangout on one of Sweet Valley's main streets. Jukebox music filled the room, background for the conversation dominated by none other than Bruce Patman.

"So next week I'm taking the black beauty down to the Mojave for another road rally. She's running so well now there's no way I can lose."

"Gee, Bruce, I'd love to watch," Jessica offered. "Can I come?"

"Sorry, baby, it's hot and dirty. You wouldn't like it." Brushing her aside, he turned to John, who was polishing off his third slice of pizza. "Say, buddy, you taking odds on the tennis regionals?"

"I'd be a fool to bet on anyone but you," John answered dryly.

"Bruce is going to win, for sure," Jessica declared, but she could have been talking to the air for all the attention she got from him.

Minutes later, Elizabeth and Todd entered Guido's. Elizabeth looked at Jessica, who was obviously feeling left out, and wondered how much longer it would take before Jessica finally woke up.

The crafty old Jessica simply didn't exist anymore. Instead, a meek, compliant young lady had taken over and was staring worshipfully at Bruce. The old Jessica would never have let a boy walk all over her like this, Elizabeth thought. And no one, not even Bruce Patman, was worth the humiliation he was putting her through.

"Ken, you doing anything tomorrow?" Bruce asked. "Dad gave me a rifle I want to try out."

"You with a gun, Bruce? You sure you can shoot that thing?"

"Anyone can hit a bunch of clay saucers. It's a skeet gun."

"Tomorrow, Bruce?" Jessica cut in. She felt him slipping away. "I thought we had a date."

"You must have your days mixed up, Jessica," he said, still looking at Ken. "So what do you say, Ken? Tomorrow afternoon?" Bruce looked at his watch. "Whoops, gang, excuse me, but I've got to make a call. Be right back."

Jessica studied her hands, tensely folded in her lap and looking like someone else's.

When he returned a few minutes later, Bruce was wearing a somber expression. "Sorry, gang, the party's over for this boy. I just called home, and Mom told me my grandmother's taken a turn for the worse. I've got to get back there."

"Bruce, that's terrible," Jessica offered quickly, aware of a vague insincerity she was feeling. "Your grandmother's been having a very rough time lately."

"Yes, she has. I knew you'd feel for her. Listen, I'll take you home first."

"You don't have to do that," called out a voice from the next table. Bruce turned around and faced Elizabeth, who continued, "Todd and I will take Jessica home. After all, Bruce," she added, her voice thick with uncharacteristic sarcasm, "I wouldn't want you to go so far out of your way."

Elizabeth thought she saw Bruce sigh with relief. "Thanks, Liz. It would make things a little easier for me, save me a little time."

"I'm sure it would, Bruce. Coming, Jessica?"

Before Jessica could protest, Elizabeth grabbed her by the arm and led her toward the exit. Jessica didn't even have a chance to give Bruce a good-night kiss.

After she led Jessica to the backseat of Todd's car, Elizabeth took Todd aside and whispered, "I've got an idea you've got to help me with."

140

"Shoot."

"I want you to drive around for a half hour. Then I'm going to come up with an excuse so that we have to come back here."

"What for?"

"Just do it, please. If I'm right, the answer will be obvious."

Todd shrugged, but agreed to go along with her plan.

After a few silent minutes in the car, Jessica finally spoke up. She was angry at her sister for having taken her away from Bruce. "I could have gone with him, you know. Our house is on his way."

"But his grandmother is sick, Jess," Elizabeth noted. "I'm sure he wanted to get back to his house as soon as he could. Besides, he didn't object to our taking you."

Halfway to the Wakefield house and right on cue, Todd spoke up. "Uh, I hope you girls don't mind if I make a stop first. I just remembered Mr. Stillman said that Jupiter and Saturn would be visible near the moon tonight. It's so clear out, I figured I'd try to spot them."

"I didn't know you were interested in astronomy, Todd," Jessica said.

"Oh, yes, ever since I got a telescope when I

was twelve," he answered quickly, coming up with the first thing that entered his mind.

Todd took his time driving up to the top of the hill overlooking Sweet Valley. He pulled off to the side of the road about a half mile from Miller's Point, the flat promontory that served as a local necking spot. The night sky was crystal clear, and they were able to see the twinkling lights of the entire valley below them. In the sky above and to the left was a creamy slice of half-moon. But there was nothing that could pass for Jupiter and Saturn.

"I'm getting bored," Jessica told Todd after five minutes of sky watching.

"Just give me a few more minutes. I know they're up there somewhere."

But five minutes more and Elizabeth could see that Jessica wasn't going to take any more stalling. She urged Todd to take them home. Ever the obliging boyfriend, Todd drove back down the hill and turned onto the street where the Wakefield girls lived.

About a block from their house Elizabeth smacked her forehead and announced, "I don't believe it. I left my keys on the table at Guido's!"

"I'll take you back," Todd offered. "Right now."

"I have my keys, Liz," Jessica said. "You can get yours tomorrow."

"No, someone might take them. I've got to get them now."

"Well, you can drop me off first, Todd. I'm tired," Jessica declared grümpily.

But Todd had already turned around and was headed back to the center of town. Jessica could only fume silently in the backseat.

If Jessica's anger was merely smoldering now, the next sight that greeted her made it blaze. When they returned to the restaurant, the black Porsche was parked right out in front.

Elizabeth's instincts had been right. "We'll be out in a minute," she told Jessica as Todd pulled in behind Bruce's car and helped her out. "Oh, look who's still here!" she added.

Jessica didn't need the prompting. Quickly recovering from her surprise at seeing the car, she announced, "I'll come in with you." She was out of the car and marching toward Guido's before Elizabeth could say a word.

As the two sisters entered the restaurant, they saw that the party was still going strong, and it looked as if they'd been the only ones to leave. Except for one person, that is, who'd also left and then returned. Only he'd brought along a visitor. Holding court at a table with Ken and John and their dates was Bruce—and an attractive redhead.

Jessica glared at the table. For a split second Elizabeth was afraid Jessica might have gone into shock, and immediately she regretted the drastic step she had taken to make her sister see the light.

But Elizabeth had underestimated her twin. Jessica wasn't in shock at all. The fog she'd been enveloped by had simply lifted, and she was now standing there looking for the first time at the real Bruce Patman. As a sly smile slowly stole over her face, she mapped out the stages of her revenge. The old Jessica was back. And Bruce Patman was finally going to see her in action.

Fourteen

Jessica marched up to the table. "Well, well, I see I'm not the only one who had a mad urge for another slice of Guido's pizza."

Bruce's face turned white at the mere sound of the voice. "Jessica, what a pleasant surprise. Uh, I'd like you to meet Aline Montgomery. She's a—a friend of the family."

"Friend?" Jessica questioned. "I'd say she looks more like a grandma to me. You did say you were going to see your grandmother, didn't you, Bruce?"

"Yeah," he admitted, "but—but—"

Ignoring him, Jessica turned her attention to the redhead. "Hi, Grandma. I see you made a quick recovery. Must be Guido's magic pizza." She picked up the pie from the table and examined it closely.

"Who would have thought this simple pizza could turn a sickly old lady into a pretty young girl?" Then she turned to Bruce. "And you, poor birthday boy. You've turned so terribly pale. It looks like you could use some of Guido's miracle cure, too. Take that, Bruce Patman!"

Before he had a chance to react, Jessica threw the gooey mixture right in his face. "And here's a little something to wash it down with." She grabbed a pitcher of soda and poured it over Bruce's head.

Bruce made a grab for Jessica's hand. "Hey, calm down, baby!"

"Don't 'baby' me, Bruce," she snapped. "Don't think I'm dumb enough to have missed the point of your little act tonight. Well, I've got a surprise for you. We're through!" As Jessica picked up another pitcher of soda from a nearby table, Bruce—in his scramble to get out of the line of fire—stumbled right into the artificial waterfall at the back of the pizzeria.

The sight of Sweet Valley's most eligible senior dripping wet and covered with pizza was too much for Jessica. She began to giggle, and soon she was nearly doubled over with laughter. After a moment of stunned silence, the rest of the crowd joined in. It was a new experience for all of them. They'd never seen Bruce Patman so humiliated by anyone.

Jessica then turned to Winston and smiled. "I believe I owe you a date," she said. "Let's go."

Taking the startled boy by the arm, she marched him out the door toward his car.

"Excuse me for one second, Win," she said once they were outside. She walked right over to the black Porsche. "I have one more bit of unfinished business to take care of." Without another word, she set about letting the air out of all four tires. Winston didn't make a move to stop her, delighted that Bruce was finally getting just what he deserved.

Back in Guido's, after the excitement had died down, Todd and Elizabeth had taken some empty seats next to Robin. Shaking his head, Todd remarked, "I'll bet anything she won't even thank you for this."

Elizabeth shrugged, unconcerned. "It doesn't matter, Todd. What's important is that the old Jessica is back—and that she had enough sense to throw Bruce Patman out of her life. That's thanks enough for me."

"Excuse me, Liz," Robin interrupted hesitantly. "I don't mean to be a pain, but . . ."

"Sure, Robin, what's up?"

"I was just wondering. . . . The Pi Beta Alpha meeting is coming up this week, and I wanted to know if you were going."

"I doubt it," Elizabeth said. "I haven't been to a meeting in ages. Matter of fact, I'd forgotten all about it."

"Gee, that's too bad."

Elizabeth looked at Robin questioningly. "Why should it matter to you if I'm at the meeting?"

"I know you don't think Jessica's been a very good friend to me, but this meeting will prove just how much of a friend she is."

"How?"

"She's going to put my name up for membership."

Elizabeth raised an eyebrow. "Are you sure?"

Robin smiled mysteriously. "She promised—and it's one promise I know she's going to keep."

Elizabeth wished Robin wouldn't put so much faith in Jessica. She was willing to bet anything her sister had no intention of keeping that promise. More times than she could remember, Jessica had told her how the chubby girl did not fit in with the sleek PBA image. Why would she do a complete about-face now and push for her membership? Elizabeth couldn't come up with a reason, and she could only figure that Jessica would conveniently forget until long after the meeting had passed, at which point she would be filled with apologies— apologies that would do Robin little good.

But Robin didn't need Jessica to pledge, Elizabeth realized. And then and there she made a decision.

"I think I'll be at that meeting after all," she told Robin. She'd be there to pick up the pieces if Jessica let down her friend. She'd nominate Robin for membership—and there would be nothing Jessica could do to stop her. It would probably throw the club, and Jessica, into an absolute uproar. But they all deserved the pressure, Elizabeth told herself, not realizing the chaos she was about to create.

Can Liz outwit her scheming twin and make Robin a Pi Beta? Find out in Sweet Valley High #4, POWER PLAY.

SWEET VALLEY HIGH

☐	26741	DOUBLE LOVE #1	$2.75
☐	26621	SECRETS #2	$2.75
☐	26627	PLAYING WITH FIRE #3	$2.75
☐	26746	POWER PLAY #4	$2.75
☐	26742	ALL NIGHT LONG #5	$2.75
☐	26813	DANGEROUS LOVE #6	$2.75
☐	26622	DEAR SISTER #7	$2.75
☐	26744	HEARTBREAKER #8	$2.75
☐	26626	RACING HEARTS #9	$2.75
☐	26620	WRONG KIND OF GIRL #10	$2.75
☐	26824	TOO GOOD TO BE TRUE #11	$2.75
☐	26688	WHEN LOVE DIES #12	$2.75
☐	26619	KIDNAPPED #13	$2.75
☐	26764	DECEPTIONS #14	$2.75
☐	26765	PROMISES #15	$2.75
☐	26740	RAGS TO RICHES #16	$2.75
☐	24723	LOVE LETTERS #17	$2.50
☐	26687	HEAD OVER HEELS #18	$2.75
☐	26823	SHOWDOWN #19	$2.75
☐	24947	CRASH LANDING! #20	$2.50

<u>Prices and availability subject to change without notice.</u>

Buy them at your local bookstore or use this convenient coupon for ordering:

Bantam Books, Inc., Dept. SVH, 414 East Golf Road, Des Plaines, Ill. 60016

Please send me the books I have checked above. I am enclosing $_____
(please add $1.50 to cover postage and handling). Send check or money order
—no cash or C.O.D.'s please.

Mr/Mrs/Miss _____

Address _____

City _____ State/Zip _____

SVH—4/87

Please allow four to six weeks for delivery. This offer expires 10/87.

A LOVE TRILOGY
First there is <u>LOVING</u>.

Meet Caitlin, gorgeous, rich charming and wild. And anything Caitlin wants she's used to getting. So when she decides that she wants handsome Jed Michaels, there's bound to be some trouble. ☐ 24716/$2.95

Then there is <u>LOVE LOST</u>.

The end of term has arrived and it looks like the summer will be a paradise. But tragedy strikes and Caitlin's world turns upside down. Will Caitlin speak up and risk sacrificing the most important thing in her life?

☐ 25130/$2.95

And at last, <u>TRUE LOVE</u>.

Things are just not going the way Caitlin had planned, and she can't seem to change them! Will it take a disaster and a near-fatality for people to see the light?

☐ 25295/$2.95

<u>Prices and availability subject to change without notice.</u>

Buy them at your local bookstore or use this handy coupon for ordering:

You're going to love
ON OUR OWN®

Now starring in a brand-new SWEET DREAMS mini-series—Jill and Toni from *Ten Boy Summer* and *The Great Boy Chase*

Is there life after high school? Best friends Jill and Toni are about to find out—on their own.

Jill goes away to school and Toni stays home, but both soon learn that college isn't all fun and games. In their new adventures both must learn to handle new feelings about love and romance.

☐	25723	#1 THE GRADUATES	$2.50
☐	25724	#2: THE TROUBLE WITH TONI	$2.50
☐	25937	#3: OUT OF LOVE	$2.50
☐	26186	#4: OLD FRIENDS, NEW FRIENDS	$2.50
☐	26034	#5: GROWING PAINS	$2.50
☐	26111	#6: BEST FRIENDS FOREVER	$2.50

ON OUR OWN—The books that begin where SWEET DREAMS leaves off.

Bantam Books presents a Super

Surprise

Three Great Sweet Dreams Special Editions

Get to know characters who are just like you and your friends . . . share the fun and excitement, the heartache and love that make their lives special.

☐ 25884 MY SECRET LOVE #1 by
      Janet Quin-Harkin. $2.95

☐ 26168 A CHANGE OF HEART #2 by
      Susan Blake. $2.95

☐ 26292 SEARCHING FOR LOVE $2.95